NIGHTGALL

They had brought him to Wheeler to take control of the dangerous streets – the famous marshal, Nightgall, feared, yet spoken of in snide whispers too. Somewhere, it was said, was a man named Burnett whom even Nightgall would not face.

If the ageing marshal knew of the tales that had followed him he gave no sign; it was enough that Liz Ellwood believed in him and that the upright Asherton, the banker, respected him.

Nor did he flinch from other, savage men who challenged his authority, those like Tyler who came at the smell of easy money in the town as the streets erupted in gunfire.

Finally, too, came Burnett, the killer, and Nightgall walked out to meet his final challenge.

By the same author

The Killings at Sligo
Ballad of the Stalking Man
A Posse from Stratton Forks
The Pistol and the Rose
The Man Out There
The Gunman from the Grave
Hanging Day
The Storekeeper of Sleeman
The Death Man
Mad John Coe
Season of Death

NIGHTCALL

LEE F. GREGSON

ROBERT HALE · LONDON

First published in Great Britain 1992

ISBN 0 7090 4761 4

Robert Hale Limited
Clerkenwell House
Clerkenwell Green
London EC1R 0HT

Photoset in North Wales by
Derek Doyle & Associates, Mold, Clwyd.
Printed and bound in Great Britain by
WBC Print Ltd, and WBC Bookbinders Ltd,
Bridgend, Glamorgan.

'Who is the tall dark man who seems to exercise such strange control over her?'
'The person to whom your worship alludes must be ... Nightgall, the chief jailer, who lately paid his suit to her. He is of a jealous and revengeful temper, and is not unlikely to take it in dudgeon that a handsome gallant should set eyes upon the object of his affection.'

William Harrison Ainsworth: *The Tower of London* (1840)

ONE

She cried out once but no one came. Struggling hopelessly she tried to break free of them, get out of the dim alley that was filled with a patchwork of deep shadows and dull yellow glows from upper windows, filled too with rising dust, the iron grips of the men, the stench of their breaths and of their bodies. No one would come in response to a sharp, high sound bursting from the throat of some woman out in the street at such an hour. Some woman not abed with her man, then, might go on crying out forever in the night in some town such as Wheeler and no one would come. Close, in the alley, struggling, gasping, then grunting – two of them there were – low-pitched words:

'Fer Jesus' sake ... *hold* the bitch!'

'Hold some of her yoreself! Git them goddam' claws still!'

Fabric tearing then, the gleam of white flesh. Gaspingly, inexorably, though perhaps surprising them at first with her animal strength, she was being moved deeper into the alley and going more

quickly now as her strength did begin to drain and theirs became fiercer and more urgent. Even so, once she snapped her forehead down and fetched a grunt of pain from one of them, whose nose immediately began to bleed.

'Yuh'll pay fer that yuh shithouse slut! By Jesus yuh'll pay fer that!'

'Keep a-hold o' her!'

'That'll earn yuh one last prod with a hot iron!'

'Take her in there.'

There was a lean-to in back of a livery where the alley ended. They did get her in there but not without further effort and noise and they did get her to the filthy earth floor and one of them, while the other locked her arms, began tearing the clothing off her.

'Git a lamp. Is there a lamp? I like to see what I'm ridin'.'

'There's no damn' lamp. Don't waste time.'

Then someone did come. Out of deep shadows, tall, in dark clothing but with a patch of white shirt gleaming and the glint of a drawn pistol being whipped across the man who was casting her clothes aside, turning his head at the last, the wrong moment, catching the cold, hard barrel in the mouth; falling away; whimpering in his throat; unable to articulate because nearly all of his teeth were smashed and his tongue was cut and gushing blood, his lips ravaged; his whole mouth, when next it would be seen in light, one glistening red-black slash. The other one let go of her and felt his diving right hand erupt with pain when the gun barrel struck it and then, having nowhere to back off to, legs spraddled, against the farther wall of the lean-to, his own scream tearing the quiet of the night as the long barrel, whipping savagely upwards, crashed into his unprotected crotch, and, as he doubled over, grasping at it as though somehow to press the agony away, receiving in his stooping face a rock-hard lifting knee.

She was almost naked, like some long white grub in the gloom, trying to crawl away, her breath rasping in and out, whimpering, her limbs quivering.

'Easy ... easy ... there's no more. They're done with. Easy ...' His leathery hands were unexpectedly gentle as he helped her to sit against the side wall but because her eyes were clouded with uncontrollable tears she could not recognize him; though she should have known him by his hard, sharp voice that could not soften even when he had been trying to comfort her. After what seemed like a long time but was only a very few moments, and while moaning, bubbling sounds came out of the darkness, she asked, 'Who are you?'

But he had to strain to understand what it was she had said. Then, 'Nightgall.'

He could not tell whether or not she had heard him for there was no response and her face, a pale, featureless oval, had sunk down. He stood up. To those barely discernible but still moaning in the darkness he said, 'I'm Nightgall, town marshal of Wheeler. Get yourselves out of here before sun-up. Let me find either of you in Wheeler again, and' – a match flared suddenly, dazzlingly – 'I'll know you again' – the light died, leaving only its own sharp tang in the nostrils – 'and I'll tear your balls out an' feed 'em to the town dogs.'

There was a rustling sound in the darkness. He had crossed to where the woman was, and in the alley's lighter darkness could be seen as a shape that was broad, tall, cradling the white shape of the woman.

A man on Main, opposite, taking the air saw him, heard his boots pounding in a measured way along the boardwalk, carrying his burden lightly, saw him cross an alley, and another, looking neither left nor right, until he came to the sun-peeled, two storey structure that was Maudie Grout's whorehouse, otherwise styled the Wheeler Hotel, and go in backwards through the outer doors and vanish.

Incongruous in the light from pink-shaded lamps he stood, still cradling the woman, blood from her spotting the worn carpet in the lobby.

'Maudie!' It was a bellow that would have been heard in all corners of the Wheeler and it fetched to the upper balustrade a pale, powdered, elfin face, to which he called, 'Tell Maudie to come down now. I've got one of hers, and tell her she'll want medicaments.'

Maudie Grout was thirty-five years old and

looked fifty, thickly powdered, rounded, the flesh under her silk wrap juddering as she came down the bare wooden stairs, serious-faced and bearing, as far as he could see, no medicaments.

'This way.' She led him, trailing her sweat-soured perfume, along a narrow passageway to a small, grimy room with a cot in it and little else. Nightgall put the woman down on the cot.

'She was in a lean-to in the alley next to Gault's with two men.'

'Who were they?'

'Couple of drifters. Nobody I'd seen before. Spent up in one o' the saloons, I'd say, an' nothin' left over for your place. She was unlucky. It must've seemed like Thanksgiving. Why was she out?'

'I didn't know she was.'

'Who is she? I've seen her, but I don't know what her name is.'

'Maggie Rorke.'

Maudie was bending over the whore on the cot, her mousy hair hanging down either side of her pouchy face.

'She's not hurt; not much.'

'She's exhausted an' got a knock on the nose an' she's scared shitless. The clothes they ripped off her are still in the lean-to. I doubt that they're worth going for, but if anybody does, don't let 'em do it before daylight.'

Maudie, wearing loose slippers, scuffed over to the door.

'Flo!' A plump girl with long dark hair and wearing a plain, faded house-dress came. 'Get some cold water in a bowl and a sponge and go up to my room and fetch the brandy.'

'Is she cut?'

'No, she's not cut, she's got a nosebleed. Go on.' With a simpering glance towards the marshal, the plump girl went. 'What did you do with them?'

'Rapped 'em around some; gave 'em the word on departure. Maudie, this time of night you have to be sure they don't go out.'

'It's this shit of a town. You sure they weren't them railroad track men?'

'No, they weren't. The town's no better an' no worse than a hundred others I could think of. Remember what I said. Goodnight Maudie.'

'Goodnight. I'm obliged to you, Marshal.'

'No, you're not,' said Nightgall. He left her and walked along the passage into the pink lobby and then out into the jagged dark of Main.

That was the cesspool, this, the promised land, even the scented bower; curtains drawn, a lamp with a lemon shade, one lamp only, casting wild shadows in a room of blessed calm.

'Coffee?'

'Yeah.' He stretched out his long legs, tossed his shallow black hat on to a sofa with clean bright covers on it. He sat then rubbing coarse fingers over his closed eyelids, a man who had been burned by fierce suns, with a deeply-seamed face that had a look of brown granite, iron-grey hair thick at the nape of his neck, an inch-long white scar under his left eye, a man with broad, flat wrists and large knuckles. He was dressed in dark pants tucked into the tops of cowman's boots, a now-soiled white shirt, a black string tie and a black vest of soft leather looped with a silver watch-chain, and on the left side of the vest, a dull metal star upon which only the letter M was any longer discernible.

'You've got spots of blood on your shirt.' He glanced down. She said, 'Leave it here. I'll clean it and wash it.' She passed through to an adjoining annexe and he could hear her preparing the coffee, clattering cups. A woman of middle height, she was finely rounded, with full lips, large dark eyes and thick black hair. She was not beautiful and no longer in the flush of her youth but there was about her a most compelling sensuality, captured sometimes in a quality of movement, a certain glance, and when she spoke, in a beguiling huskiness of voice. Liz Ellwood, the solitary outsider admitted to the guarded, private world of Nightgall. She came back.

'Here.' He took the cup she held out. She curled into a wide chair opposite him, legs up under her, tucked her wine-coloured robe around them. 'Corrado's saloon?'

Sipping at the rich, restoring coffee, he was enjoying the sight of her over the rim of the cup.

'Nope, not this time. Two pilgrims. Got a-hold of one of Maudie Grout's girls. Could've turned real nasty. It was bad enough as it was.'

'What was she doing, out?' He shrugged. 'Did you take her back there?' He continued sipping the coffee, looking at her. She said, 'I'm sorry.'

'They didn't even have the courtesy to offer.'

She had a low, musical laugh and her eyes shone, searching his ravaged, serious, leathery face as he leaned forward to put the cup on the floor. Liz got up out of her chair, took the cup and carried it into the annexe. When she came back, almost silently in her soft moccasins, she crossed to the lamp and turned it low, then stood holding one cool, cream hand towards him.

A faint pearly light bisected curtains that were not quite closed, in the hush of very early morning. Inside the room objects were not clearly defined, all edges brushed with shadows.

When he crossed over the border of sleep to a warm half-wakefulness, he saw first the blood-streaked face of the whore; but when he blinked eyes that were still glued with sleep she receded, then vanished and became the face of *The Blue Boy,* enclosed in a cheap gilt frame on the wall, opposite. Under the covers he stretched his long legs and became aware of the woman's arm resting across him. Slowly he turned his head on the pillow. It was a rounded, creamy arm, limp in sleep, a loving, not a possessive arm. She drew a breath in through her delicate nostrils, expelled it long and gently through her mouth, moaned then, softly, worked her cheek deeper into the pillow, a mass of dark hair spilling over it and over her face.

With fastidious care, so that he would not disturb her rest, Nightgall slid his legs out of the bed, set his feet on the mat beside it, stood up, naked, and padded cat-like around the end of the iron bedstead collecting up his boots and his clothing. The clothes he tucked under one arm, then scooped up his heavy, holstered pistol and the thick shellbelt, and all of these things he carried out of the room and down the worn carpet of the stairs and into the parlour. There, he dressed in longjohns, pants, socks and boots and slipped his black leather vest over his bare torso. The blood-flecked, soiled white shirt he left over the back of a chair. He rolled the shellbelt around pistol and holster to be carried in that way in one hand, dropped his shallow-crowned hat on to his head, leather thongs hanging free on either side of his lined face and went out by the back door into Wheeler's pale dawn.

A town of some size, it stood now upon the brink of change, for at last the railroad was coming, the gangers laying the steel rails now only a matter of twenty miles or so to the north, men who were to be seen on occasions now in Wheeler, that being, by a small margin, the nearest town to their present operations. Already Nightgall had had to sort out some problems between these men from the railroad construction gang and cowhands who, over years, had traditionally come in, and he had thought dourly that such friction, fueled by drinking, would probably get worse before it got better. Now he walked along the alley alongside Liz Ellwood's house and the shop that belonged to her that formed the front portion of the building, facing on to Main, an establishment dedicated to the sale of women's clothing. Whenever he looked at the place, her name above the door, he could not avoid a sense of guilt, though Liz herself would always choke him off whenever he tried to express it openly. For he was well aware that, though her small enterprise did well, there were some among the womenfolk of Wheeler who disdained to enter it, and almost certainly that was because of Nightgall. For though he and Liz Ellwood, for some time anyway, had practised the utmost discretion, their relationship had long ago become common knowledge in and around the town and they had long since become resigned to that fact. From time to time he had made attempts, albeit not strenuous ones, to offer her a chance to end it.

'I'll keep away. Say the word an' I'll stop coming here.'

'It's a touch late for that don't you think? Besides, that's not what I want.'

Now he glanced up and down what seemed to be a deserted Main, then crossed it obliquely, heading towards the Wheeler jail and marshal's office behind which were his own living-quarters.

Inside, he dumped pistol and shellbelt on a table, hung his hat on a peg behind the door, then checked upstairs where, on occasions he slept; then all through the downstairs, for he was a cautious man, moving on past the two steel-barred cells into the front office with its battered desk and gunrack. He passed back along the passage beside the cells, dim places that sometimes smelled of stale liquour, tobacco smoke, human sweat, disinfectant and urine, and at times a gut-tearing combination of all these things. Today, though, there was little more than a damp, sour smell about them.

He fetched a large, rough towel, a clean shirt and a razor, some soap and a tin mug and went out into the yard where there was a barn and a privy and a lean-to containing a tin bath and a large round copper with a blackened chimney pipe that passed through the roof. From a pump in a small adjoining outbuilding he levered water into a pail and one after another, poured several pails into the copper; then he lit the fire beneath the copper and blue smoke went climbing into the grey, windless morning. When the water began to steam, he dipped some out in the tin mug, set up a small piece of mirror and soap-lathered his stubbly jaw with his fingers. By the time the water was ready to be baled into the bath, he had finished shaving. He carried heated water into the bathtub, fetching a pail of cold from the pumphouse to temper it, then stripped and presently washed away dirt and blood, the rank smell of the men, the stale perfume of the whore, the sweeter, fainter perfume of Liz, and her warm, sharp woman-smell, ashamed at having carried the other foul traces into the cleanliness of her bed.

This time, after he had dressed, he walked back inside and unrolled the shellbelt and looped it around himself and buckled it; then he thonged the lower end of the holster to his right leg, and when he straightened up, the plain wooden steel-centred butt of the big pistol tended to jut out a little from his thigh. He went through some slight hitching and twisting actions with belt and holster, once half drawing the pistol, settling it back into leather again until he was perfectly satisfied with the balance and feel of the weapon at his side. From the tall, naked, muscular, sinewy but anonymous man stepping out of the bathtub he had now once again become Nightgall, the Wheeler marshal. Presently he prepared a breakfast of thick slabs of bacon. eggs, coarse brown bread and coffee and when he had finished the meal, stacked cup, plate, pan and utensils into a chipped enamel bowl, carried it out to the lean-to and baled into it the remaining hot water from the copper whose fire was now but bright embers. When the dishes had been washed and dried and put back in the house, he returned to the lean-to and dragged the slopping bathtub across the yard and, tipping it, poured the soapy water into a deep sump-hole; then he fetched a pail of cold water from the pumphouse and swilled it around the tub before stowing it in the lean-to.

Long bright fingers of sunlight were now reaching out across Wheeler; threads of blue smoke were beginning to stand up into a lightening, hazy blue sky from chimney pipes all over town. Nightgall prepared to make his first official appearance on Main. Before he did, however, he again crossed his own yard and opened the doors of the barn. He smoothed a hand down the sleek neck of the handsome black horse, tipping more feed into its trough and making sure there was plenty of water in the other trough. Then he walked out and through the yard and up the alley that led on to Main.

A shiny-skinned, balding man, a swamper at Juan Corrado's saloon, the Silver Cat, departed from the still-steaming boardwalk, mop in one hand, pail in the other, and re-entered the gloom of the Silver Cat, a place that was still rank with smoke and liquor and, despite his early morning labours, the sourness of vomit. The floor had been mopped, the chairs lifted down again, the tables wiped, the spittoons cleaned and the lamps refilled, and now the swamper laid aside mop and pail and held a match to a short black cheroot. A bar-dog, broad-faced, jowly, wearing a once-white apron, was engaged in slowly polishing the long bar with a soft yellow cloth. Deep blue smoke now drifted around the swamper's head.

'Seen the marshal. Seen Nightgall.'

The bar-dog did not pause in his slow rubbing of the polished wood, but glanced up.

'Now?'

'Earlier. Come out o' the alley by the Ellwood woman's shop. Come stalkin' right out like a goddamn' tomcat along a fence.'

The bar-dog chuckled, rolled his eyes.

'Aye-yi-yi-yi! An' a right comely li'l tabby she is!'

'Then you tell me, Ed, how come some ol' bastard like that gits his boots slung under a cot like that.'

'Ah, but he ain't just some ol' bastard, he's Nightgall.' The swamper inhaled, then exhaled a stream of sweet-smelling smoke towards the shadowed, almost invisible ceiling. 'An' was I you,' the bar-dog said, 'I wouldn't even say thoughts like that out loud.' The swamper made a wry face, flicked ash into his pail of grimy water, then he picked up pail and mop and went off into the deeper, farther reaches of the long room.

'Nightgall. I hear what I hear.' The remark trailed behind him after he had disappeared and the bar-dog paused a moment then continued his slow but purposeful polishing. The swamper could think and even say whatever he had a mind to, or was foolish enough to, but the bar-dog, long ago, in towns not unlike Wheeler had been made into a cautious man who therefore knew when it was prudent to hold his tongue.

* * *

Liz Ellwood came moaning softly out of sleep and in the earliest moments of awareness reached out an arm and, sliding it lazily about, discovered that she was alone. Breathing gently, still yielding limply to the enclosing warmth of the bed, she nonetheless opened her dark eyes and in the glow of daylight through curtains, saw that his clothes had gone. She allowed her mind to go back over the hours and it was then, unexpectedly, that she recalled that he had for once made no mention of Dobrey. Now, still sleepy, her mind not yet functioning sharply, she could not immediately decide whether that was good or bad. Perhaps he now regarded that matter as closed, though her next thought was that it was surely not in his brooding nature to do so. Neither could she decide, as indeed she had never been able to, whether his declared attitude to Dobrey was based upon the celebrated lawman's nose he sometimes spoke about, or whether it was simply a case of very old-fashioned jealousy. That hardly seemed in his nature either. Yet there were some things about which Nightgall was not able to be persuaded as, to her frustration, she had long ago had to accept. Thinking about it had brought her more fully awake and soon she rolled over, hauled herself up on her elbows and lay against the pillows, her nightgown clinging to the warm dampness of her body. He would have slipped from her bed in the early dawn, taking care not to disturb her. He would have dressed downstairs, perhaps, then returned to where he lived, behind the Wheeler jail. She set her small feet on the floor, reached for her robe, and tying it at her narrow waist, walked across to the windows and drew one of the curtains to one side, looking out from over her shop, across Main. Somewhere down behind the jail there rose a slim ribbon of smoke from a chimney pipe, and Liz smiled slightly, knowing it would be from the copper in which he would have heated water for his tub. She let the curtain fall back into place, slid her feet into her moccasins and went downstairs. She was all too well aware that people gossiped about her and Nightgall, though of course, in the nature of such things, nothing was ever said directly; but there was enough in a half-heard word, conversations abruptly discontinued, and sidelong glances, for her to know of it, and she more than suspected that there were those who would never be seen inside her shop because of it. Well, that was unpleasant but so be it. She was her own woman. She had known him for almost a year, in fact since he had first come to Wheeler, brought there rather, by an ad hoc committee of townsmen as a replacement for a marshal who had been more often drunk than sober and consequently had lost control of the streets. Nightgall, it was said, would only have to put in an appearance on those same streets to settle things down, and that had proved to be virtually the case. There were still untoward incidents like the one that had occurred last night, and there were, as was to be expected, some drunken fights and some incidents of bloodletting; but control was gradually being re-established. It would never be total, Nightgall or no Nightgall, but then this was a town in a rough country and on occasions it gave shelter to some wild men. A marshal had to do the best he could; but he must at the very least do that. And Nightgall had. Yet she had heard other things, too, a little later, after his appearance in Wheeler, no more than hints, whispers, certainly nothing said to the man himself or to her, and she had chosen to close her mind to them. If there was anything to tell, he would do it himself in his own good time. Or not.

They were in a grimy room at the back of Gollin's Trading. Gollin himself there now, more than a touch jumpy, anxious, and one of them lying on a bench that had been pulled a short way out from the wall, in a tight foetal attitude, his face still grey with pain; dried black blood on him, on his face, all over his dirty blue shirt-front, and his right hand no more than one blue and purple swelling. Yet he was the better off of the two. Someone had put a rolled-up blanket on a trestle-table and the other man was lying with one temple resting on it, his body also in a somewhat tucked-up posture, broad hands held up to a face which at first glance appeared to be no more than a mask of blood. Blood, some freshly bright, some turned black, and saliva, smeared his grubby, pinkish woollen vest. His lips had swollen to several times their normal size and from between them still oozed a reddish, gelatinous slime. Stokes and Petch their names were, and they were still in Wheeler; they were at Gollin's. Gollin himself continued to be serious, very nervous, asking repeatedly who had brought them there and not getting answers. When there arose some sort of stirring out in the nearby passageway, Gollin spun around as though he had been jabbed with something sharp.

'Who's that? Who's there?'

Crake, the seedy odd-job-man who was with Gollin, said, 'It's all right, it's only Evans.'

After a muttering in the passageway where another of Gollin's men was at that particular time, a short, plump individual with unkempt dark hair showing from beneath a filthy derby hat which once had been a light sand colour, and perhaps even fashionable somewhere, a man in cord pants whose belly under his grey shirt hung out over his belt buckle, came sidling in. He smelled strongly of wake-up sweat, stale whiskey-breath, and mothballs, and he had not yet shaved, a fierce black stubble darkening jaw and cheeks. Nobody mentioned who had sent for Evans, either, and now Gollin did not even bother to enquire. Clearly, Evans did not wish to be here, involved, and neither did Gollin want any part of it. Somehow both seemed to have become aware that Nightgall had ordered these two hurt men out of Wheeler.

Evans stood inside the dusty room looking unhappily from one injured man to the other. There was a single window, closed, the glass opaque with grime, but Gollin had gone to it a number of times and tried to peer through it, though these actions arose more from his jumpiness than from any hope of being able to see anything. He was doing it again now, and without turning, said to Evans, 'Now you're here you'd best take a look.'

When Evans spoke it was in an unexpectedly – almost incongruously – deeply-pitched voice and in the accents of a cultivated man.

'I seriously doubt that there will be very much that I can do ...' He trailed off uncertainly. It was the man with the smashed mouth that he was looking at, though he had not approached him closely. Petch, on the table, was moaning faintly, his eyes closed, perhaps unaware – even in his agony, uncaring – that there were others in the room. 'The mouth,' Evans continued, 'is much too badly swollen to permit proper examination.' He opened and closed his own lips stickily, and added, 'I could perhaps get him something for the pain.'

'I want him – both of 'em – out of here,' said Gollin to nobody in particular. He wanted Evans and his peculiar odour out of there too, but he said, 'Fetch ... whatever it is, then.' Evans turned to leave. 'Make sure that long bastard don't see you while you're about it. I don't want this place connected.' Evans left. To Crake, who would have gone sliding out with Evans, Gollin said, 'Where the hell are *you* goin'? You stay right in here. As soon as that smelly little prick gets back an' does what he does, you get these two buzzards out. You. That don't mean half the damn' outfit carryin' 'em, neither.'

Crake licked his lips, spread his hands.

'It warn't me, Gol. I mean, that brung 'em.'

'I don't care what you didn't do. What I'm saying' is what you are gonna do is get shut of 'em.' He turned sharply. Evans was back. 'Ain't you gone yet? What now?'

Evans looked at the floor, the useless window, the moaning man on the table, the man scrooched up on the bench, anywhere but at Gollin, but he said:

'The medicament ... I don't have very much and it was costly. There is the matter, therefore, of payment ...'

'Jesus Christ man, it's not my problem!' Gollin said. He jerked his head. 'They don't look like they'd be flush, I'll grant you. But I ain't payin' that's certain.'

Evans nodded vaguely, looked as though he might still hang around, then went shuffling through the door and there came again a muttering of voices. Evans did not reappear for a matter of some fifteen minutes. When he did, he was looking marginally more pleased with life and he had brought with him a capacious leather bag.

'The question of payment,' Evans said, 'has now happily been resolved.'

'Has it now?' said Gollin. 'An' who the hell by, might I ask?'

Evans managed to find room for his bag on the table alongside the groaning man, opened it and looked speculatively at its contents.

'I regret I am not at liberty to say.'

'Oh, don't mind me then,' said Gollin. 'They're only here on my damn' premises, an' without my say-so!'

Then from somewhere out in the passageway, somebody called out that Nightgall was now out, on Main.

TWO

Nightgall was indeed on Main for a time but soon wandered away down a sidestreet to stand for a few minutes watching the men who were part-way through building the railroad depot, their hammering and sawing having become familiar background noises in Wheeler this past week. After the years of talk about one day the railroad coming through Wheeler, here indeed was hard evidence that at long last the promise was to become reality. Nightgall pursed his lips and could not help wondering what new problems this long-awaited advance might bring to him as the marshal, after the sounds of the construction workers were no more than a memory. Eventually he turned and walked away back up the street in the direction of Main. When he reached it he acknowledged people he found there, and they him. He knew too, that as he watched, he in turn was watched, but that did not disturb him at any time, provided the peace was kept.

At one point he revisited the alley and the place

that had been the scene of the disturbance on the previous night. Maggie Rorke's ripped clothing lay scattered there, some of it dirty and flecked with blood. Coming out again, Nightgall wondered idly where the two of them had got to, reasoning that in all probability it was not out of Wheeler, anyway, not just yet, in spite of what he had said to them; they had been too badly beaten. Crawled off somewhere. Taken in somewhere. Well, when they could, they would either vanish or they would surface on one of the streets, and if they did that, then they would hear from him again. He glanced along towards Liz Ellwood's shop but it was not yet open. Nightgall returned to the office in front of the jail.

Ash Dobrey now stood near the window of a room over Corrado's saloon. A man above average height with an almost handsome face, he had light-coloured hair, thick over his ears. He was dressed in grey pants and a grey shirt with narrow white stripes down, and when he was at the card tables, wore a cravat of dark blue or deep red. Over the shirt he customarily had on a dark grey, silver-figured waistcoat. Always armed, Dobrey was, though not with a heavy pistol. Worn on the left side just below the hip-bone, in a tan, tooled-leather holster, he carried, butt foremost, a .38 calibre pistol of British make, the barrel of which had been shortened; thus it was essentially a very short range weapon. However, as Dobrey had been heard to remark, albeit somewhat wryly, 'My enemies, when they see fit to appear, tend all to be at short range.' A sardonic, deceptively relaxed man, Dobrey worked card tables at the Silver Cat on a percentage deal with Corrado, and seemed to do well enough out of it. A good man to get along with, so went the word, and a dangerous enemy.

Dobrey had noticed Nightgall on Main, but it did not matter now, for Dobrey had already been out and about in Wheeler and was now preparing to go downstairs again, this time to his breakfast and was feeling mildly satisfied with at least some matters of concern to him. Yet he, too, before he withdrew from the window, looked along towards Liz Ellwood's shop, took note that its front door was still unopened.

In the sour back room of Gollin's Trading Company, Gollin had again confronted Crake.

'Where are they?'

'In the barn.'

'Christ! An' their horses?'

'In there too, Gol.'

'It's still too close, Crake, an' it's still my damn' barn. Give 'em a few hours, then as soon as it's dark, git 'em on their way. I want *shut* of 'em. Understood?'

'Yeah.'

'An' Crake ...'

'Yeah?'

'Who knows about these jaspers apart from Evans an' some o' the boys here?'

Crake did not want to look directly at him but knew he would not be able to avoid it.

'Dobrey, I reckon. He was about, earlier, anyway, but he won't give Nightgall the nod, not him.'

Likely that was true enough, even in this town, Gollin thought, but at the same time it made him nervous, knowing that someone outside Gollin's Trading had got to know that they had been there. Immediately it involved *him* and he did not wish to be involved. He now wondered if it had been Dobrey who had given money to Evans for he could not think of anyone else likely to have any, or enough to give, and if Dobrey had done it, why would he have done so? That was the trouble in this damn' place, a man never knew what was going on under the brooding surface. To Crake he said, 'If ever I do find out who it was fetched 'em here in the first place, I'll make the bastard answer for it. I ain't done with that yet.' He turned but paused as he was about to leave. 'There's this blood in here, too. Git some water an' clean it up afore you do anything else. Scrub it away real good. By Christ, I don't need none o' this, no way!'

When, at a little after ten o'clock that night Gollin himself went down to the barn and lit a lamp, neither men nor horses were there. Awkwardly, he climbed the ladder into the loft just to make sure that some smart alec had not simply led the mounts away but allowed the men to remain, then, satisfied, came down and for a few minutes moved about stroking and gently slapping the two sleek horses that belonged to him. Then he went outside. Crake was at the back door of Gollin's, framed in yellow light, one hand held to his forehead, peering out.

'I tol' yuh they'd gone,' he said when he saw who it was and would have said some more but Gollin sharply waved him to silence.

'I don't want to know, Crake. They've gone. Let 'em stay gone.'

Nightgall, in the course of his day had passed a word or two with a fair number of people in Wheeler. Some, he knew, were wary of him, some were likely even afraid of him, but there were a few, as there would be anywhere, who sought to curry favour, so eventually Nightgall came to know that his two night vultures, at least for a time, had been kept at Gollin's and he knew, also, that they had now gone from there. Once, in passing, he saw the smooth, tall gambling man, Dobrey, walking with his easy gait along the opposite boardwalk. Maybe he was strolling along on his way to pay a call on Liz Ellwood, for Nightgall knew that sometimes he did, and that she in turn was cordial to him, but in a careful way, withdrawn, too. When, some while ago, she had told Nightgall that Dobrey did come to the shop sometimes, to chat, unfeignedly attracted to her, Nightgall had surprised her by saying that he already knew.

'And you don't *mind*?'

'I mind. You know I mind. But don't you spit in Dobrey's eye for the sake of it. Don't be taken in by that smile he puts on. Sure, be polite, but always stay just out of reach. He's a hard man, is Dobrey.'

'He'd not struck me at all in that way.'

'Maybe he hasn't, but you hear what I say Liz. Try not to give him cause for resentment. He's a cold and dangerous man, never mind appearances.'

'What if he should push too hard?'

'Unless I misread him, he won't do that. Not while I'm still here.'

It was not until after he had gone that she had realized the significance of all that he had said. It was then that a slight shudder passed through her, of the kind that folk half-joke about when they say that someone, somewhere, has walked across their grave.

Gollin, much relieved now, hands in his pants pockets, stood at the mouth of the alley that ran alongside his place of business, listening to the night sounds from the saloons along Main, seeing the few people on the boardwalks passing in and out of lamplight. He did not hear or see Nightgall, however, until the marshal spoke to him and then his knees near to buckled with shock. Nightgall, however, made no apology.

'Evening, Gollin.'

'Uh ... Marshal. I didn't hear yuh. All quiet?'

'Looks like.'

'Yeah. Yeah.'

'Mind you,' Nightgall remarked, 'looks can deceive. A man can't be too careful.'

'No.'

'No. Especially in a job like mine. Never can tell for certain who's for an' who's against.'

'No ... I guess.'

With one thumb Nightgall pushed his hat back slightly.

'Goodnight, Gollin.'

''Night Marshal.'

So that would sweat Gollin for a while, have him keep his miserable little head down.

At the corner of Main and one of the intersecting streets, touching his hat to a man and woman going by, arms linked, he paused to speak also to Asherton, a middle-aged, narrow-shouldered man, cleanly and neatly dressed, with a pearl grey hat set just-so on his iron-grey head. Asherton the banker.

'Good evening, Mr Nightgall.'

'Good evening, Mr Asherton. I don't often see you out as late as this.'

'That's true,' said Asherton. 'Just taking the air for a while, after a meeting.' That would have been a Wheeler Town Committee meeting, for sure. 'Any problems tonight, Marshal?'

Nightgall shook his head gently.

'A couple of the railroad men got in somethin' of a shindy, earlier, down outside Frater's. Nothin' special.'

Asherton nodded, blue smoke curling.

'Then I take it we can all rest easy, Marshal.'

'You can rest easy.'

'Goodnight then, Mr Nightgall.'

'Goodnight Mr Asherton.'

A touching of hats, then moving in different directions.

Nightgall heard the singer before he saw him, then strolled along to take a closer look. Passers-by were smiling. A deep, rich, clear voice, drunk but intelligible, was carrying far along Main.

'... *nor shall my sword sleep in my hand,*
'Til we have built Jeru-salem
In England's green and pleasant land!'

'Evenin' there, Mr Evans.'

'What—? Oh. Oh, Marshal.' He was swaying, studiously drunk, shabby, short, thrust-bellied, exuding his unappealing scent of liquor and mothballs.

'On your way home then, Mr Evans?'

'Home? Indeed. Indeed I am, Marshal. Home.'

'Then go with care,' said Nightgall.

The plump man nodded then lurched suddenly into the black mouth of a yard and began retching deeply. Nightgall turned away from the quick sour stench and went on his way. A sad, pathetic man, was Evans. Nightgall had come across others of his ilk all across the west and he suspected that each and every one of them had a story, but that it was probably the same one. A different thing though, tonight, about Evans. For a good long while he had been sober, only because he had had no money to buy liquor. Tonight he had been singing drunk. His fortunes must have changed for the better, an unusual circumstance, in Wheeler.

Sometimes, in a room off an alley in the run-down hotel known as Frater's, men gathered around a table topped with blue and white checkered oil-cloth, under a single lamp, to play cards. Nondescript men they were usually, in greasy clothes and none too clean – clothes or men; some who did odd jobs around Wheeler when they had to, or had no job at all, and on occasions, by the happenstance of meetings and laconic exchanges, others came to chew the fat and watch the game, maybe sit in from time to time, drifters, stage-line men stopping over – though soon there would be fewer of these now that the railroad was coming. When he could manage to get a night off, Court, one of the bar-dogs from Corrado's Silver Cat would come to look on, and if he could persuade her, fetched Polly Marchant who also worked, when she had to, at Corrado's.

Court was in there now with her, Polly wearing a bright yellow dress that hugged her narrow torso and small breasts and clung tightly around her hips. The room, even with its single window partly raised, was rich with the smells of human bodies, cigar smoke and Polly Marchant's cheap scent and powder and the stench of the alley beyond the black window, and alive with buzzing flies. Moths fluttered around the lamp. On a small table against a wall stood some bottles and shot-glasses. The once-bright, now creased and grimy playing cards were flicked and shuffled in yellow light as the four around the table played a desultory game of five-card stud. Nobody with much money, little, therefore, to stimulate the game. Hole cards down, now each with three face-cards in the light, arms reaching, dropping chips into the pot, one man dropping out bunching his cards together, three continuing, the dealer flicking out the cards for the final round, the fourth face-card to each remaining player, and then the bets were in again after that go-round. The showdown; hole-cards being turned over, fetching a whiskery grin from a man they called Rube, who raked in the final pot. Between hands, stretching limbs, scratching damp armpits, taking a drink, exchanging muttered comments, laughing a little; Court with his left hand down behind Polly, squeezing a firm, rounded buttock gently, she giving him a look but not moving away, either.

'Nightgall run two pilgrims out last night,' said somebody, yawning the words. 'They beat some whore from Maudie's so I heerd.'

Maggie Rorke. Polly Marchant knew her slightly. She said nothing, though. Someone else said, 'Way I heerd it, Nightgall bust 'em up pretty bad, but nobody saw what happened to 'em, after.'

Polly Marchant leaned a little more against Court while his hand worked absently at her buttock. He could feel her warm breath on his neck. One or two of them there in the room nudged each other and grinned but neither Court nor Polly seemed to notice, or if they did, didn't care. One thing that Court did know though, was that even while she was with him it would be Dobrey she would be mooning over, but Dobrey had his own eyes turned elsewhere.

'One day,' a card player said, 'someone's gonna come along an' stop that Nightgall's clock.'

'Well, it won't be me,' somebody else remarked and there was a murmur of laughter.

A player with spiky whiskers all around his mouth, the man called Rube, his broken, brown teeth showing, said, 'Mebbe some day somebody is gonna ask the man hisself if what they say is true.'

'That won't be me, neither,' the other man said and this time the laughter was more full-bodied.

'If what's true?' asked Polly Marchant, standing slightly away from Court as the faces all turned towards her.

'Some say,' Rube said, 'that Nightgall, the great Nightgall, turned tail an' lit out from some place called Argon, three year or so back. Feller named Burnett faced 'im down.'

'Who says that?'

A shrug. 'One an' another.'

'It proves nothing if it's only talk.'

'What's the matter Polly? Yuh got the hots fer Nightgall?'

'No!'

Court was not amused by this turn, flushing but saying nothing.

'Jes' as well, I'd say Pol. Gits his boots off at Liz Ellwood's, does Nightgall. Ev'body knows that.'

Now Polly Marchant was not amused, face stiffening. Someone else said, 'Well I reckon it's all shit about Nightgall. He's killed men, he has, an' that we all do know. He's a hard bastard.'

'Somebody did face 'im down. Burnett.'

'Then I don't care to meet Burnett.'

'Are we gonna deal up agin or sit here jawin' about some damn' gawky Texan come out o' nowhere?'

'Was fetched.'

'Fetched, then.'

'Who's in an' who's out?'

Polly Marchant was still pouting but made no objection when Court put his hand on her backside again and then put his mouth close to her ear. She glanced at him, made a face that he could read and together, as the card game started up afresh, went through an inner door trailing a roll of curly smoke after them. After a moment the card players under the lamp paused, grinning, hearing steps going up bare wooden stairs, then a door closing.

THREE

Day by day, on the surface, especially in places like Wheeler, everything remained just as it was yesterday and prospects seemed to be that nothing would change tomorrow either, or ever. But even in Wheeler appearances could be deceptive. Nothing ever remained quite the same and Nightgall, though he was well aware of undercurrents, must simply go on acting out his given part, apparently expecting no change, yet waiting patiently for it to come.

'Did he visit you again? Dobrey?' He had begun the day by promising himself that he would not ask that question, but the moment he saw her again, that particular resolve went right out of the window.

'Yes, he came to the shop, but there was scarcely any talk possible. Other people were here. Women.'

'He's got more nerve than I have, anyway, just comin' in.'

She laughed softly, her eyes shining, her dark

hair swinging forward when she kissed his forehead as he sat in one of her comfortable chairs. Then she was serious, kneeling on the floor, resting against his leg.

'I've heard ... those men ... they didn't leave Wheeler right away. Is it true? They might have gone by this time though.'

'They might have. They were hurt too bad at first. They were up at Gollin's for a time, right after, but not now.'

'Did you talk with Gollin?'

'He knows that I know. That's enough for the present.'

'You're a somewhat deep man, Marshal Nightgall.'

'That's what they say.'

'We're in the wrong places. I should be in the chair, you on your knees, saying: "Let me carry you away from here." '

'If I did that, where would we go in this territory, that I wouldn't have to say it all over in six months?'

Now she laughed outright, her head back, then after a moment, got up and curled herself in his lap.

'You *could* carry me off, Marshal. See? There's not much of me.'

'There's just enough of you,' said Nightgall.

Outside, not far away, in a sharply-cut obsidian shadow, someone drew on a cigar and for an instant the roseate glow from it etched out the features of Ash Dobrey. He waited. A lamp went out in one room, another came on upstairs and presently went out. Dobrey turned and walked away.

Days went by. The railroad depot was nearing completion. More of the railroad men were putting in appearances in Wheeler, and Nightgall was sometimes caused problems because of it. It was noticeable, too, that he had begun to move with some care. What was not known was that it stemmed more than anything else from a feeling he had, a most odd feeling, as though he might have heard, carried on the very wind, a whisper of enmity, a precise threat of danger. Nightgall had no belief whatsoever in sixth sense but he did have a profound belief in the duplicity of his fellow-men when motivated by hatred or jealousy or money, or elements of all of these things. He mentioned nothing of this to Liz Ellwood but she knew it simply by looking at him, sensed it and taxed him with it.

'No, there's nothing, Liz.'

'Something is not right. I know it. Is it something about *them*? Is it the men you hurt?'

He shrugged. There was no point in further denial.

'Maybe. I've not yet sighted them. I did have word a while back that they'd not gone far. I don't understand it Liz, that part. They picked the wrong time an' the wrong town an' they got hurt, an' I wouldn't have said they were the sort to push it further.'

'Please ... take care.' As soon as she had uttered them she knew that the words must sound foolish. 'I mean ...'

But he said, 'I know what you mean.'

When, only a few days later, in early evening, one of them – it was the one called Stokes – briefly showed his face to Nightgall, it was clear that the move, whatever it was, was on.

It was at a spot at the far end of Wheeler near a jumble of small buildings, some of them long disused, and a livery with a corral out back of it, and further back yet, a barn which had a loft with no door on it. No sooner had Stokes appeared for a moment in a gap between two buildings, however, than he withdrew hurriedly and vanished and seemingly in some alarm when he saw Nightgall down towards the corral. Using normal caution, Nightgall first glanced behind him, but the sprinkling of people abroad seemed not to have noticed Stokes. Nightgall felt uneasy for he did not believe that his sighting of the man had been accidental; in his expression there had been the flash of something else that was not quite right, something false. Nightgall walked slowly along the way Stokes had gone and when he arrived at the corral saw that it held five horses, all peaceable, and that beyond the corral, across some open ground stood a barn with an open loft. Nightgall stood still, looking at the barn and looking in particular at the dark rectangle where the loft door ought to have been. Of his quarry there was no sign.

Liz Ellwood swished a broom over the boardwalk outside her shop, glanced up and down Main, then went inside. She closed the shop door and slid the bolts home and passed through another door and along a passage to the living-quarters where she set about preparing supper, taking pains over it, knowing that Nightgall was to come. As she went about her task she thought about him and about whatever it was he might be brooding over. Wheeler had been a busier place of late, and she knew that Nightgall had had to take a hand in several skirmishes involving railroad construction men, and men from the cattle ranches, but she was certain that it was not these things which were overly concerning him, and not necessarily the men he had beaten, either. A man hard to draw out, was Nightgall, even for this woman, close as they had become. There were some faint rumours too, still. She would have had to have been completely without wits not to know that. Rumours about his past. People, in their nature, had made sure that she was aware of the talk through the occasional enigmatic comment. Once, in her own shop, she had challenged another woman over an acidic remark made just too audibly, and that exchange had ended with the woman stalking out, probably never to come back. Generally though, there was a reluctance on the part of those who gossiped to come right out with it; a human, if unappealing propensity for innuendo rather than outright honest statement. She had said nothing to Nightgall of any barbs she had endured, for it would only have angered him, perhaps even have driven him away and she did not want that now. She was comfortable with him. Dobrey was another matter entirely. Not by the merest word or gesture had the gambling man overstepped the mark, yet he had become something of a problem, for clearly he admired her and equally clearly would not easily be turned away. And restrained and courteous though he had been, there was something present behind the expression in his eyes which flickered now and again, something frightening. She had heard what Nightgall had said of the man and had taken due notice of it. She would try not to give offence to Dobrey but she would take care never to allow him to come too close.

While Liz Ellwood was occupying herself in her kitchen as the hour for supper drew nearer and the light was fading, the whole town had quietened too, and Nightgall felt, just for a moment, that he must be the only living creature in all of Wheeler. He was no longer standing near the corral, looking towards the barn, but had carefully and quietly retraced his steps, made his way along Main and down the alley and stood still, now, at the mouth of a yard behind the

Wheeler whorehouse. Slowly he rubbed his coarse hands against his pants at the thighs, drying away any vestige of sweat on the skin. He was further away and was seeing it from a different angle but he no longer had his attention fixed on the dark opening to the loft. True, it had drawn his eye the instant he had seen it, just as they had known it would, and he now considered that he might have been but a minute or two from death if he had moved out towards it. The light was poor and he thought they had chosen their time well; poor light, a quiet hour, Nightgall out and alone.

Somewhere behind him he heard the faintest of clicks and he moved with surprising speed to one side, turning in the same motion and by the time he was fully turned the long pistol was in his hand, tilted upwards, Nightgall facing the back of the whorehouse.

Maudie Grout herself was out on the back porch, her pale face showing almost startlingly above a dark wrap. Fingers were up to her lips, her other hand making pointing motions to the back of the feed and grain next door to the Wheeler Hotel. Then she held up one finger. One man only. Nightgall showed two fingers. Where was the second man? She shrugged, shook her head, turned and vanished inside the house with no sound.

Nightgall paced slowly along towards the back of the feed and grain where there was also a yard of sorts, and inside it a jumble of rotting sacks, some lumber, a buckboard and a broken wagon. He took good care in setting his boot down after each step and when he reached the opening to the yard he waited a tense second or two, then ran in, bent double, shouting, 'Now, you bastard!' His sudden and noisy entry startled the man Stokes – for it was Stokes – half-risen from where he had been crouching by the tilted-over wagon, and he gave a cry, raising a pistol and Nightgall, still moving forward, fired the big pistol in his own hand with a sound like a thunderclap in the evening stillness and Stokes screamed when he was hit, plunging backwards, striking against the side of the wagon. Nightgall kept right on moving, going down, rolling, hearing the booming explosion of another pistol somewhere behind him, and when he came to his knees, turning, dust coming down on him from the dry boards of the feed and grain where Petch's slug had banged in right above him. He shot with a lifting barrel at the second man in the opening to the yard, come from Christ-knew-where while Nightgall had been going in at Stokes, and even as he saw Petch hit, jack-knifing, shot at him again and heard that one hit with a slap, and saw Petch driven back, something spraying from the side of his head, and then he was down, drawing great noisy, hoarse breaths, his body, on its back, quivering and trying to move, and failing.

Nightgall was in over the top of Stokes first, the barrel of the long pistol at the man's mouth.

Stokes was not dead but was in poor shape, the front of his shirt, at the breastbone, sodden with thick blood. Lamps were coming on in the whorehouse next door, at the back windows, and somebody, a woman, called, 'Marshal?'

Nightgall called back, 'It's all clear! Send for Evans!'

In nearby parts of Wheeler, at the sound of the gunfire, people had stopped whatever they were doing. The few citizens on Main at that hour paused and looked down towards the Wheeler Hotel where the shots seemed to have come from. A bar-dog in an apron came out through the batwings of the Silver Cat and looked around, seeing nothing. Upstairs, Dobrey turned down the lamp, raised his window and stood in the gloom looking out over Main, where there were few lamps, and some that had been glowing had been turned down. At the other end of Main, in the kitchen where Liz Ellwood was, the sounds had not been nearly as loud, but it had been no less certain what they were. She stood at her bench, now hearing only the clock ticking, clenched hands resting on the smooth wood, head bowed, her whole body tense. She drew three or four very deep breaths, willing the tension to drain away. Once, he had said to her: *'If there's gunfire, never go to find out where it is or what it's about. Wait 'til I come.'* It was no good though. She had to go outside, find out if anyone knew what was happening.

Standing on the boardwalk just outside the shop, she saw in the evening's pearly dimness a few folk on the move, others standing around uncertainly, then caught sight of someone running awkwardly, as though unused to it. A woman, she thought, and called, 'What's happening?'

But there was no answer and whoever she was, a plump girl who had come from the direction of the Wheeler Hotel, turned and vanished down an alleyway. Further off somebody called something but she could not hear what was said. When a man she recognized, from a freight office, went running along the opposite boardwalk, she called, 'What is it? What's happening?'

He scarcely paused but called back, 'Two men down, they reckon, shot, back o' the Wheeler somewheres.' *Oh God no. Not him. Don't let it be him.* She was wiping her hands on her apron without realizing that she was doing it. She remembered again, though, that he had been firm, almost brusque about it, his face like tanned leather in the lamplight: '*If there's gunfire, never go to find out where it is or what it's about. Wait 'til I come.*'

She turned and went slowly back inside the darkened shop and for the second time that evening, slid the bolts home.

After a little while, when there was no more shooting, a few windows and doors began to be opened and some men approached the yard at the back of the feed and grain.

Nightgall shouted, 'Somebody get some lamps!

There's two men shot. Somebody's gone for Evans.' He hoped that that was so. In fact the upshot of his call to the woman at the Wheeler had been that the plump girl from Maudie Grout's had gone out by the doors on Main and shambled off in search of the man. In a very few minutes several lamps appeared, glowing unnaturally in the early evening, bobbing along behind the Wheeler towards where one of the shot men lay. Nightgall was there. When they got a look at the man, who was lying on his back near the entrance to the feed and grain yard, somebody said, 'Jesus!'

One of Nightgall's slugs had struck him in the belly and there was a fist-like bulge of something at the wound, the other high on the cheekbone below the left eye, and all of the side of his head had been pulped and the eye itself was hanging down in the mess. With some difficulty Nightgall went through the man's pockets and withdrew money from one of them, leaving a watch where it was.

'There's another man down near that wagon,' said Nightgall and lamps were carried there; but they could hear him before they reached him, his harsh, bubbling breaths, as though he was trying to get rid of whatever was inside him by hawking it up. His head was tilted against the one good wagon wheel, the upper part of his shirt a red and black mass from the bad wound there and from a mixture of blood and saliva from his mouth. He was not dead but he was not far from it. In the yellow smear of lamplight Nightgall went down on one knee and though it was impossible to know whether or not the man still had any awareness, said, 'Can you hear?'

The eyes were glazed and the blood-laden breathing continued but there was nothing else. Evans did not come, and even if he had done so, as Nightgall and others could perceive, there would have been nothing that he or anyone else could have done. Even as they stood watching, the man's head slid further down against the wheel, and about then, all sounds ceased. Nightgall did not immediately rise from his kneeling position but, as he had done with the one at the entrance to the yard, searched the pockets and eventually withdrew money.

'We can forget about Evans, anyway, and fetch Anstiss.' Anstiss was the undertaker. Rising, Nightgall saw that the town committeeman, Asherton, wearing no hat and in shirtsleeves, was now there. Nightgall handed him all of the money he had taken from the dead men. 'If you wouldn't mind, Mr Asherton. Some of it ought to be for Anstiss, for the burials, the remainder, whatever the Town Committee wants to do with it.'

Asherton nodded. 'It's probably the fairest thing at that, Marshal. But this is a lot of money. There must be more than three hundred dollars here. Who were they?'

'They were the two that had got hold of the girl from Maudie Grout's. They were saddlebums.

They likely tried for the girl because they had no money for the whorehouse. They've struck it real lucky somewhere in a real short time.' Asherton looked at him silently as though trying to draw more from him about the inference but Nightgall's face was completely without expression. When he spoke again Asherton realized that it was to somebody else among the dozen or so men who had now gathered there. 'They been in at your tables?'

Faces turned. Dobrey, in grey pants, white shirt and blue string tie, with expander armbands on his shirtsleeves, shook his head briefly, smiling faintly.

'They're not known to me.'

'Well,' said Nightgall easily, 'they were sure as hell known to somebody in this town. Maybe a dangerous friend to have, considerin' the state of 'em now.'

'What exactly happened, Marshal?' Asherton asked.

'This one,' Nightgall said, 'made sure I saw him and knew I'd recognized him, drew me down here probably to give the other one a clear back-shot. It went wrong, but not by much.'

Asherton looked at him palely under the lamps.

'It seems a hard revenge for them to have tried, Mr Nightgall, if that's what it was intended to be.'

'It does that,' said Nightgall. Someone called out that Evans would not be coming. It seemed that the girl had found him but had been unable to wake him. 'Now, there's another one,' said Nightgall to nobody in particular, 'that's come into recent money.' He eased his way through the group and left. Anstiss was just arriving.

Liz was standing under a hung lamp in her porch when he came, dusty and dishevelled, and she bowed her dark head aginst his chest when he held her arms and he could feel the tremors running through her warmth, faint pulses at his fingers.

'I'm sorry Liz. I should have sent word as soon as I could.'

'I thought ...'

'I know. I'm sorry,' he said again. They went inside.

FOUR

The railroad tracks were now but a few miles short of Wheeler and because of the proximity of workers, the town was noticeably busier. The traders there were beginning to smile and certainly the saloon-keepers were, even the swarthy, brittle-tempered Corrado seeming more agreeable. Money was changing hands freely in Wheeler, across counters, across the long, polished bars and ebbing and flowing on card tables; at Maudie Grout's Wheeler Hotel it had become a happy and noisy boom-time.

The dessicated Anstiss, with the help of a lay preacher named Bowden, had seen to the burial of the dead; no one else, apart from some layabouts paid to carry the boxes, attended the proceedings. By the time the fine white dust had begun to stir across the burial mounds, the companions in life and now in eternity, Stokes and Petch, were soon forgotten. Nightgall, as it happened, never had learned their names. Now he had another matter to concern him, for at least some of the money coming into Wheeler was finding its way to the bank and he felt impelled to speak to Asherton about that. The banker was inclined to take notice of Nightgall for he had been a prime lobbyist in bringing him to Wheeler in the first place and customarily he was prepared to back his own judgement. So now he looked at the big, darkly-clad man seriously.

'Does it concern you that much? Do you see a real danger?'

'Sooner or later,' said Nightgall, 'when there is enough money, enough bait, somebody just won't be able to resist. That's my belief.' They were in Nightgall's office, to which place they had strolled after meeting in the street. Asherton took off his hat and put it on the old desk, sat down on a bare wooden chair nearby and smoothed both of his hands slowly over his short, greying hair. Nightgall put one boot on his own chair behind the desk and leaned folded arms on the raised knee. 'I know the place is as secure as it's ever had to be,' he said. 'It's a good bank, well built, and so on. But men who are determined enough, or desperate enough, would come when the doors were open, when people are in there; customers. I know there's never been an attempt before, but you've got a whole lot more temptation in there now.'

'I want to transfer some of the funds to the bank in Coleman,' said Asherton, 'but I'd rather not do it by stage. I'd thought to wait until the railroad reaches us. Miles assures me that it will be in no more than ten days. The inaugural link with Coleman will take place almost immediately, even before the track is laid out beyond Wheeler. Money could be sent then in a secure van, properly guarded.' Miles was the railroad man in charge of laying the track, a large, unexcitable man who, when the occasion arose, could help put a halter on the rowdiest of his wild boys.

'If there should be a try for the bank before that can be done,' said Nightgall, 'what are your people likely to do?'

'On my explicit orders,' said Asherton, 'in the event of a hold-up, they are not to offer resistance, invite shooting.'

Nightgall looked at him levelly and nodded. Asherton did not let it go at that. 'There's something more, though, isn't there Mr Nightgall, for you to raise this?'

Nightgall pursed his lips.

'Yes and no. Something and nothing. Yesterday, when I looked in at Corrado's I noticed a man named Tyler. Tall, thin feller, sallow, pocked skin. He's known to me.'

'For what reason?'

'Armed and violent robbery of a stage down near Perrault, some few years back. We took Tyler a week later, along with an accomplice. Tyler did seven years for that, an' was lucky the stage guard lived.'

Asherton raised his white eyebrows a fraction.

'I see.'

'As I said,' Nightgall repeated, 'something an' nothing.'

'Did he see you?'

'It didn't seem so, not even by the twitch of an eyelid. Yeah, he saw me.'

'Might that make the difference, if he'd come into Wheeler as an oppportunist, smelling money?'

'Maybe,' said Nightgall, 'maybe not. They're a strange breed, these bastards. They've got a nigh-unshakeable belief in their own ability, even when it's gone bad for 'em in the past. In general they reckon it was all somebody else's fault, never their own. Doesn't seem to matter how many times it's gone sour, back they come. So I don't know that it would make that much difference to somebody like Tyler. But there's another thing, probably more important. If it should be that he does make a try for the bank, he'll not be alone on the day. Yesterday he was alone.'

'Are you saying, then, that an attempt is probably unlikely?'

'I'm saying he was alone yesterday, that's all.'

Asherton rubbed a pale hand around his jaw.

'Will you talk with this man, maybe move him on?'

'I'll have a word. Move him on? I don't know. While he's in sight, at least I know where he is. If I moved him on, he could always come back, sudden, any time he felt like it. I don't know. I'll think about it. And I'll do what I can to watch the bank until you can unload some of the money, safely.'

'Thank you; and for the warning about this Mr Nightgall.'

Nightgall nodded and Asherton left.

Of Nightgall, to acquaintances in Corrado's, Tyler said, 'I *owe* that long dark bastard.'

'So did two other *hombres* they jes' finished throwin' sand on.'

Tyler wiped his mouth with the back of his hand.

'There's them that Nightgall will face,' he said, 'an' there's them that he'd rather not face.' A man in a grey suit and with a black string tie and pure white shirt turned to look at him, offered a drink, and when it had been poured, nodded towards his private table, one that was covered with green baize.

'Come take the weight off, friend.' They moved away together through a crowd that was increasing, under the press of many voices. Polly Marchant in a pale mauve dress trimmed with blue and white, watched Dobrey, not recognizing the sallow, scarred man who was with him, or indeed paying him much attention. Court, working with two other bar-dogs, moving back and forth behind the long counter, when he could, glanced in the great, ornate mirror, keeping his eye on Polly, noticing Dobrey and realizing that she had fixed her attention on the tall, lean gambler. Blue smoke went curling under the hanging lamps. The big saloon was becoming alive with movement and rich with laughter. A piano man in a red shirt was trilling disjointedly over in one corner, the sounds making scarcely any impression under the collective voices. A busy evening in the Silver Cat. Corrado himself, dark in his silver waistcoat, stogie between his teeth, was moving casually, easily about through the throng, pausing sometimes for a word with someone, always watchful. An evening for watching.

Later, Nightgall moved along Main, also watching and listening. He had paused for a moment when he heard shouting and scuffling down one of the sidestreets, near a lumber yard, and settled his hat more firmly on his head and walked with his long, easy strides towards where, it seemed, two or perhaps three dark figures were grappling, lurching back and forth. This sort of thing had become a not too uncommon occurrence in recent times. A bottle crashed and splintered against a stack of lumber. Curses rent the night air. Nightgall lengthened his stride. He could not see them at all clearly against the night and risked that they would see him coming against the faint glow along the street, from Main. They saw him right enough. Four paces short of them – there were two men only, and he could smell them before he distinguished their number – the scuffling ceased abruptly and they closed on Nightgall. Knuckles skidded off his left cheekbone and now the rank smell of sweat and liquor was very close around him as he went backing off, the men coming at him purposefully. His reflexes were still surprisingly good but the first blow had made him blink, and now they were crowding him too close for him to draw the pistol. He could not see whether or not they were armed. Nightgall lashed out his left fist and it thumped against a face in the gloom, fetching a sharp cry. But there was to be no miracle this night, for there were two of them, hard and powerful, and that was one too many and he was no longer young. He put up a good showing though and had the satisfaction of knowing that he hurt both of them before he went down and one of them kicked him in the head and it was some while before he knew anything else.

He had got as far as Liz Ellwood's place, thankful that he had encountered no one else on the way there. He was now in one of her capacious, soft chairs and Liz, with a bowl of warm water and a sponge, her dark hair loose about her shoulders, her face wet with quiet tears, was working gently, wiping away dust and blood, then dabbing with a soft dry cloth. His shirt was torn and his dark clothing covered in white dust and she thought that at this moment he looked very old. She fetched a jar of salve and began smearing it over the cleaned gashes in his leathery skin. Once, he looked her full in the eyes.

'Don't waste your tears.'

She pushed at his head almost roughly.

'You're ...' She stopped short.

'Too old?'

'No.'

'Too slow, then, or too gullible, or a bit of both?'

'No,'

'Too easy bruised.' There was no smile and his eyes glittered.

'Who were they? Were they railroad men?'

He shrugged. 'Couldn't tell. But whoever they were they sucked me right in. Five years back – no, two – I'd have drawn first and then gone in. Somewhere along the line I've turned into a stupid old man, Liz.'

'Stop it.' He regarded her narrowly. It had been an unaccustomed tone. She looked confused under his gaze, then said, 'You'd best get that shirt off. I'll see if it can be mended.' She was now being brisk, practical, but he did know that she was badly frightened and he wanted to reach out to her, but it was not the moment.

'I've got to go,' he said.

'You can't. Not again. You need to rest.'

'There's something else,' he said, 'that I need to do more than that.' Stiffly – for he was unsuccessful in concealing it – he rose from the chair, reached for his hat. His left knee hurt him too, but he made quite certain that he did not allow her to become aware of that.

'How long will you be gone? Will you come back here, after?'

'I'll come,' he said. 'Give me an hour.' He glanced down at his ragged shirt. 'I'll fetch this back with me.'

When he left the warmth of Liz's room he went directly to his own quarters behind the jail. There he changed into another shirt, another pair of dark pants, carefully brushed his black waistcoat and shrugged it on again, took a critical look at his own ravaged features in a mirror, flexed his left knee, grimacing at the needling pain there when he did it, then turned the lamp down and went out again.

He went pacing along the boardwalks of Main much as he had been doing earlier, but this time keeping as much in the shadows as he could, down one side of the street and then up the other, seeing and inevitably being seen, exchanging a word or two occasionally. He kept to one of his usual routines. He looked in at a couple of saloons, heads turning in his direction as always, and when he came to Corrado's Silver Cat, pushed on in through the batwings and made an unhurried tour, pausing at one point to speak to Corrado himself. Some conversations faltered, then picked up again when it was clear that the marshal was not seeking anyone in particular, but was here simply on one of his routine visits, and games resumed; but Nightgall knew nonetheless that every eye, at some time, was on him.

'Quiet night, Marshal?'

'One of the better ones,' said Nightgall evenly.

If the small, sharp eyes in Corrado's swarthy face rested on Nightgall's freshly-salved cuts a touch longer than ordinarily they might have done, the owner of the Silver Cat was careful to pass no comment about them. Nightgall left Corrado and moved on by Dobrey's table. No cards were lying on the green baize at present; only two shot-glasses stood there. Dobrey sat staring up at the tall man, no liking whatsoever in his expression, while Tyler was looking down at the table, perhaps hoping that he would not be drawn into a conversation.

'You're a hell of a long way from home, Tyler.'

'That's as may be,' Tyler said. He looked up then, pocked face greasy under the lamps; his green, gold-flecked eyes unfriendly. 'But where I happen to be at any time is my business, Nightgall.'

'Until it should become mine,' said Nightgall. 'Take right good care that it doesn't.'

If Tyler had been of a mind to say more he was not given the opportunity for the big, dark man who had been standing over him had given him what he had plainly regarded as the last word and had turned away and was working his way back through the crowd towards the door.

Outside, and once beyond the spill of light from the saloon's lamps, Nightgall found that he had to pause. He leaned one hand against a wall, the other lifting to his forehead while he stood blinking his eyes. For a chilling instant when he had been inside Corrado's, his sight had blurred, then cleared again, and now momentarily, it had blurred again. He shoved away from the wall and continued on his way, thankful that the purpose of his tour of Main had been accomplished. Whoever they had been, the two men who had attacked him, it was highly probable that they would either have seen him out and about or would soon become aware that, in spite of what had occurred, the reality was that Nightgall, calm and easy as ever, had apparently shrugged off his injuries and overcome his pain. That was the message that he had delivered to them. Briefly he went back to his own place and there picked up his ripped shirt and carried it across to Liz Ellwood's.

It was while she was making coffee that she heard him stumble against a chair and when she went back into the room, found him standing with one hand on his head, slightly stooped, then hurriedly straightening and saying that he was all right. At once she persuaded him to sit down and when he had done so, looked again at the gashes on his head and at his eyes. He passed the matter off as dizziness and failed to tell her of blurred vision.

Polly Marchant stepped out of the pale mauve dress, then stooped and picked it up and shook it, then hung it in the closet. One by one then, she removed each of her undergarments, unpinned and shook out her rich, reddish-brown hair and admired herself in the long mirror on the back of the open closet door; firm, small breasts she had, but beautifully formed, and a slim waist, and when she turned a little sideways, showed to advantage her neat, rounded buttocks, so much admired by Court. She sighed and reached down a long, cream coloured robe, slipped it on and, gathering up her discarded clothes, dropped them into a large wicker basket. Her poky room was on the second floor of the Silver Cat, a place now fallen relatively quiet, no heavy roar of voices from below, no tinny piano, only the occasional sound of doors closing, of footfalls going by, a woman's laughter. Bess Olford's room was the next one and from in there she could hear muffled voices, the dropping of boots on the floor, and presently the rhythmic sound of bedsprings. She would be half-drunk, Bess, and would have fetched up some foul-smelling cowboy; poor old Bess, poor hapless, hopeless diseased old Bess. Oh well, whoever he was he would find that out soon enough. One of Bess's had come back, months later, looking to break her mouth and cause her certain other injuries, mostly for old time's sake, but had made the mistake of bragging about the prospect beforehand, and instead, had got the barrel of Nightgall's pistol in his own mouth, so that was the end of that. But Nightgall had had a word with Evans, apparently to see if something could be done for Bess before, as Nightgall had somewhat indelicately phrased it, she gave the goddamn' clap to half the county. Nobody seemed to know what Evans had said to that, and anyway, nothing had come of it.

Polly walked across and raised the shade and looked out over Main. Few people were down there now and most of the lamps had gone out. If she had expected – hoped – to see Dobrey walking by then she was to be disappointed, but she did know that he had gone out, for while she had still been downstairs she had seen him leaving, his pearl-grey hat on and a cigar between his teeth. Out for a stroll in the clean night air, out, maybe, to visit Liz Ellwood for all Polly knew, or at least to hang around down there. He did do that sometimes. Once, while Court had been drunk, she had slipped out after Dobrey had gone and from a safe distance she had seen him standing across the street from the woman's shop, watching when a light had come on in an upper window. She wondered if Nightgall knew about it. Now she drew her robe more firmly around her slim shoulders, repressing a cold shudder. Nightgall. There was something about the man that frightened her. She wondered what it had been that he had said, earlier, to the man who had been sitting at Dobrey's table and whose name, she had heard later, was Tyler. Known to Nightgall. Was there anybody who was *not* known to Nightgall? Prosperity was attracting all kinds of people into Wheeler though, some of them strange and dangerous men. Like the albino dressed in ragged range clothing, hung with a large pistol, greasy, wide-brimmed hat pushed back to reveal his startling, soft white hair, his unbelievably pink eyes covertly examining everybody in the long bar mirror; watching Polly herself, sometimes, looking speculatively at her body, and looking at Dobrey and at others; at Tyler. A few minutes after Tyler had stood up and walked out of Corrado's the albino had finished his own drink and eased on out too. She drew the shade. A woman's voice cried out once, then all sounds from next door ceased. Her own door opened and Court came in. He had been drinking, she could see by the flush in his face, but he was not drunk. He paused after he had closed the door and made a motion with his head.

'Bess got some poor bastard in there?'

'By the sounds.'

Court looked at her.

'What's up? What's the matter?'

'Nothing.'

'No? Yuh got yer hang-dog face on, Pol. One o' them damn' railroaders give yuh a touch? That it?'

'No.'

'No? Well then, it's got to be ol' card-shark. Hey? Card-shark?'

'No.'

He came nearer.

'Been moonin' out the window? Too bad. He's mebbe down there right now puttin' it to Lizzie

Ellwood.' She shrugged, refusing to be provoked. 'Card-shark. Bed-bug. Whatever. Yuh still got the hots fer the bastard, Pol, I can tell.'

She shook her head. It was no use arguing with him when he was in this sort of humour.

'No.'

'Yes!' He had taken hold of the tie at her narrow middle and pulled it undone and when he pushed the robe off her shoulders it slipped to the floor and lay around her feet. 'Pure ivory,' said Court. 'My, yuh're a fine lookin' woman, Polly.' She did not want him. Not tonight. She was tired of his sneering coarseness and his roughness with her and the way he smelled. She flinched from his hand under her belly and he seized her by the upper arms, gripping tightly until she cried out, but he gripped all the harder and began to shake her back and forth with great violence, her hair spilling in disarray over her face and he went on shaking her until she began to moan and to try to free herself.

'Let ... me ... go!'

He did. Quite suddenly, and as she swayed before him he whipped one hand in an arc and caught the side of her face with a sound like a small calibre pistol going off. Her lower lip bled.

'Card-shark. Git on the bed.' Sleepwalking, holding her mouth, she did. She would rather have had him properly drunk, not half-way. He was always much worse, half-way. Undressing, Court hopped awkwardly, dragging a sock off and bumped against a wall and realizing where he was, began banging a fist on it. 'Hey there Bess, yuh diseased ol' slut! Now yuh jes' listen to this, like how a pro-fessional goes about it!' When he came naked to Polly's bed he was shaking with internal laughter. 'Now that,' he said, his anger seemingly evaporated, 'should give 'em somethin' to chew on.'

Polly thought, Oh Christ, here we go.

Downstairs in his office at the back of the building, Corrado was stacking banded wads of bills into his steel floor-safe and considered that soon he might need to send the overflow to the Wheeler bank. It was not an arrangement he would have chosen for he did not like the prissy-mouthed Asherton, but before long he would have no option. The sooner the damn' railroad reached Wheeler the better. Corrado thought that a man might do worse than buy shares in the railroad. He heard the sound of a side door opening and closing and went to look.

'Oh, it's you.'

Dobrey came in, dropped his hat on Corrado's desk and sat down in one of the padded chairs.

'A man called Tyler was here.'

'That pock-marked *hombre*?'

Dobrey nodded. 'Nightgall stopped by the table and put some weight on him. I don't know what it was about. Something way back. Tyler says it was no mistake about Nightgall leaving Argon in a rush, shit-scared of this man Burnett.'

'I've heard that before,' Corrado said. 'I'm

startin' to hear it too often for it not to be true. Still, as the man said, put it to Nightgall straight, an' see what happens.' He propped his thick body against the desk, lit a slim black cheroot, breathed blue smoke at the ceiling. 'What did he know about Burnett? Tyler.'

'Not much. Young, he said. Early thirties. Very hard. Very quick to the pistol, Tyler said, but he didn't know where he sprung from. But wherever it was and whoever he is he took a dead set against Nightgall, and Nightgall wanted no part of him.'

'Nightgall's gettin' old.'

'Not too old to blow out the lamps of those two *hombres* out back of Maudie's.'

Corrado shrugged. 'We'll never know what really went on back there, only what Nightgall hisself *says* went on.' From his pants pocket he took a bunch of keys, then walked across, bent, and locked the safe. 'Where's Burnett now? Did Tyler say that?'

Dobrey gave a non-committal movement of his head. 'Still somewhere around Argon, he thought. Got some woman there. But Tyler swears Burnett would kill Nightgall if he could be sure where he was.'

Corrado pocketed his keys.

'Nightgall's been in some sort o' ruckus by the looks.' Dobrey merely glanced down, his mouth set firmly, and Corrado, reading it, chewing smoke, let out a sharp laugh. 'But it ain't done him a whole lot o' damage. I hope yuh told 'em to light out real sudden!' When Dobrey still failed to comment, Corrado said, 'Well, I reckon they must've made a real pig's ear of it. What was it supposed to be about? The woman?' He thought it had been a stupid and even futile move for Dobrey to have made, and it could have been all over Wheeler by now. If Dobrey had thought he might drive off a man like Nightgall, in spite of all the rumours, with a couple of drunks, he must be badly astray in his reading of the man, but at the same time it was strange what some men would do on account of a particular woman.

'My business,' said Dobrey finally.

'She ain't worth it,' Corrado said flatly. 'Not none of 'em are. Yuh might jes' as well git yourself a handful o' Polly Marchant. Gawd knows she's allers flauntin' it in front o' yuh plain enough.'

'I'm not interested in leftovers from the likes of Bill Court.'

'Oh, she's a right handsome gal is Polly Marchant. Them in the back room at Frater's reckon she don't half make the bedsprings go.'

'I'll bide my time,' Dobrey said. 'I'll get Liz Ellwood yet, you see if I don't.'

'Not as long as Nightgall's still in the picture,' said Corrado, 'an' not if yuh're relyin' on the likes o' them two oafs to soften him up.' He squinted at Dobrey with his pouched little eyes. 'Are they still in Wheeler?'

Dobrey shook his head. He was not enjoying

Corrado's poking about in his personal affairs and could have well done without his unsought advice.

'Gone south.'

'It's a mercy,' Corrado commented. Suddenly he grinned, showing very white teeth and waved the half-smoked cheroot casually. 'Now the man yuh *need,*' he said, laughing and coughing at the same time, 'is that there hard-nose in Argon. Sounds like he'd clear the damn' field for yuh in short order, if what this Tyler says is true.' Dobrey flushed and looked shifty as though he might have been caught kneeling at the safe, and Corrado thought, well now, I wonder if he really would?

FIVE

It was time to close up the shop. It had been a busy day, for the town was now coming alive with people, many of them from the surrounding country, and all because the long-awaited railroad had reached out as far as Wheeler. Two women whom Liz had thought were to be her last customers for the day had just departed when a slim girl wearing a short, light green cape loosely over a pale green dress, a girl with goldy-brown hair pulled into a bun at her neck, came in almost hesitantly. Liz knew who she was; apparently she worked up at Corrado's saloon and her name was Polly Marchant.

Although Liz had already turned some of the lamps down the girl moved around the shop slowly, looking at the merchandise, seeming not to know what it was she was seeking. Then at last, in a slightly husky voice, she asked to see some particular type of dress material and when Liz lifted a half bolt of it on to the counter, looked at it and did not look at it, fingering it almost absently. Liz could see that her eyes were overly bright and were red-rimmed from recent crying, but told herself that whatever was the matter was nothing at all to do with her. She asked Polly Marchant if there was anything else that she could show her. The girl shook her head, lowered her eyes, then looked again at the cloth, touched it once more, turned away, but it was to hide the fact that there were tears again. In her compassion, her resolve of a moment ago weakening, Liz walked slowly around the end of the counter.

'What is it? Can I do anything?'

Still turned away, looking down, Polly shook her head almost violently.

'No!'

'Look at me,' said Liz. Another shake of the head. Liz thought for a moment then walked around her, took her face gently between her hands and tilted it upward. 'Look at me. Tell me what it is.' Tears were streaked down the girl's cheeks. Liz reached across and turned up a lamp. Now she was sure. There was a dried split in Polly Marchant's lower lip and a puffiness there. 'Who did this to you?'

'Nobody you know.'

'Tell me.'

'Why? So you can play milady an' set your tame marshal on him? That wouldn't do no good.' Liz, unknowing, had placed her hands on the other girl's upper arms and at that Polly flinched and tried to draw away.

'What is it? Are you hurt there?'

For a moment it seemed that she would not answer, then wordlessly she loosened her cape, then undid the cuff of one sleeve of the green dress and pushed it all the way up. The bruises stood out as ugly black blotches on her lovely ivory skin. It was perfectly clear that she had been held there in a fierce grip. Still not wanting to meet Liz's eyes she let the sleeve down again and fastened it.

'Don't you tell nobody about that.'

'But no one has the right to ...'

'Don't you *tell* nobody!'

'All right. All right, I won't.'

'Not Nightgall. Not nobody.'

'All right. But will you tell *me* who it was did this to you?'

'Why? What good would that do? None, that's what. Don't you know that if you're a woman in the saloons you got to take that sometimes? An' worse than that. Take it an' keep your mouth shut.'

'No.' Liz shook her dark head. 'No, you don't have to, Polly.'

'You know my name? How do you know what my name is? People been talkin' about me down here?'

'No, nobody has, I promise. I don't know where or how I got to know who you are, but I've been here a good long while and so have you. It just happens. Nobody talked about you here.'

'Some of them snob women that come in here wouldn't give the likes of me the time of day.'

'Some of the women in Wheeler prefer not to

come into my shop,' Liz said calmly, 'for what are maybe not so different reasons. Did you know that?'

Polly Marchant looked at her as though not knowing whether or not to believe that. She took out a small handkerchief and dabbed at the wetness on her cheeks. She seemed calmer now.

'Who did do that to you, Polly?'

'If I told you who it was you'd be real surprised.'

'Would I?'

'Oh yes, you'd be real surprised.' She walked back to the counter and began fingering the dress material. 'This is nice stuff. Nice.' She looked up abruptly. 'Does your marshal know this place is watched? Your place? At night. The part where you live.'

Liz considered whether she ought to end this conversation now, but she said, 'Is that what you came here to say, Polly, to tell me that?'

'No. Yes. Maybe it was.'

'Why?'

'Don't you *mind* bein' watched?'

'It would depend on who was watching and why they were doing it.'

Polly looked full at her, then down again as though trying to decide if she should say more.

'He comes down here, I reckon, to see you.'

'Who? Who is it you say comes here?' She thought she knew that already but wanted to hear it from Polly Marchant.

'You know.'

It was like trying to catch a quick little fish with bare hands.

'Polly, why are you saying this to me?'

'This,' Polly said, touching a long white finger to her damaged lip. 'This, he done. An' the marks on my arms.'

'Is this the same man? Is this what you're telling me? The one you say comes and watches me also did that to you?'

Polly stood twitching a corner of the dress material in her slim little fingers.

'You know who he is, but I can't say for fear of him finding out. If he found I come here, then the next time he might cut me.'

Liz realized that she was standing with every muscle tense, and that as Polly had been talking, her own mouth had gone quite dry.

'You can't mean that. Surely ...' It was suddenly very frightening. She wished Nightgall would come.

'He might. He would. He'd do it. It wouldn't mean nothin' to him. You don't *know* him.'

'If this is true you should tell the marshal.'

'No!' She looked like a startled animal caught in sudden light.

'Then tell me who this man is.'

Polly sniffed and dabbed at her puffy face again with her totally inadequate handkerchief.

'His name is Ash Dobrey.'

A small silence fell between them.

'I see.'

'Yeah, him. I know he does come here. I bet you thought that because he talks so good that he's a real gentleman. Well, he ain't.'

'I truly hadn't thought about it Polly.'

'Oh, he wants you, Dobrey does. He wants you *bad*. An' one day, or more like one night, he'll come. When it gets too much. What he wants, he takes. He waits an' he watches. He'll do that a while, an' then when you're on your own ...'

'I'm not afraid of anybody like Mr Dobrey,' Liz said, but in spite of the calm way that she spoke, the way she controlled her voice, she felt a quite odd sensation, not raw fear as such, but a kind of unreality, as though she had been exposed to an aspect of life which was abhorrent to her and that she did not want to dwell on. 'But I'm obliged to you for warning me.'

'You don't believe me, do you?'

'I believe you.'

'You don't tell him. You don't tell nobody. Especially you don't tell Nightgall. Promise me that. Promise again.'

Suddenly Liz felt trapped, drained and angry, but trapped. In the finish, she felt she had no option but to agree.

'Very well, I promise. But you listen to me now, Polly. If Ash Dobrey comes here, comes near me when Nightgall is away and I have any trouble with him; if I ask him to go and he won't go, then there's an end to that promise. Do you understand that?'

Polly with her still-damp face looked at her for a moment resentfully, then, accepting it, nodded. She turned and hurried out of the shop. Slowly Liz reached across and turned the bright lamp down.

The albino had disappeared. He had gone, it seemed, as quickly and as quietly as he had come. Nightgall, one way and another, had heard about him at the time and regretted that he had not at least caught sight of him. For a little while he had been sufficiently interested to make a few enquiries. He had even questioned the nervous man, Gollin, who it was said generally knew who was who in Wheeler at any given time, but he had drawn a blank.

'Never set eyes on nobody like that,' Gollin had said.

'Gollin,' Nightgall had observed laconically, 'you know what? You're slipping. From a man once reckoned to be well in the know, you're gettin' to be famous for the people you haven't seen.'

The exchange with the fearsome Nightgall had both annoyed and worried Gollin but had not altered the case. Yet the trader, in his turn, had seen fit to question Crake about the albino. Crake, who had still been watching his P's and Q's after the other business over Stokes and Petch, had been grateful that this time he could speak truthfully, and in nearly the same words that Gollin had used to Nightgall.

'Never heerd o' nobody like that in Wheeler, Gol.'

Anyway, the strange rider was soon enough forgotten. The event which had now captured the interest and fired the imagination of every man woman and child in Wheeler, and for that matter, many miles around, was the railroad. The shining steel rails had not only reached the town, but for the final fifty yards a double track had been laid, with sets of points, and at the extremity of the rails a shallow excavation made and a turntable constructed so that the locomotive and tender could be turned around. For the moment, Wheeler was the end of the line and it would be some months before the track would reach out to join another at Bensonville. The depot was all ready for business and the water tower, having been got into place, standing starkly against the delft blue sky, was now in the process of being filled from the Arrow river, the heavy containers of water being fetched from there on flat-decked wagons, and then hauled up by a system of beams, ropes and pulleys. All of these unusual activities drew many curious onlookers and from Nightgall's point of view, that in itself was useful, for it enabled him to cast an eye over a good number of people in the same place at the same time, some of them strangers. The Town Committee had co-opted another group of townsfolk to help with preparations for the historic day, and on a certain Saturday morning, folk from ranches and from homesteads all along the Arrow and even out as far as the smoky foothills of the Hoyt Range, began arriving in wagons, on buckboards and on horseback to discover that the unremarkable town of Wheeler had been transformed; and it was fluttering with banners and hung with bright bunting and all of Wheeler had flung open its doors for business for extended hours, and business was booming as it had not done in living memory.

At 10.40 a.m. the operator at the Wheeler telegraph, a skinny man with a green eyeshade, came out of his poky office and at a shambling run went looking for Asherton the chairman of the Wheeler Town Committee, to bring him the good news that the first train into Wheeler, the one that would be carrying officials from the railroad company and which would include a special, secure and guarded van in which money from the Wheeler bank and from anywhere else that wanted to do it, could be shipped out safely, would, within the hour, pull out of the next and larger town, Coleman, and would by best estimates reach Wheeler a little before 1 p.m.

Earlier that same day, Nightgall, still broodingly anxious, made it his business to try to find out where Tyler had got to, for he too had dropped from sight. It proved to be no simple matter. Nightgall, not unexpectedly, started down at Maudie Grout's whorehouse. Earlier still, with a lop-sided smile, he had remarked to Liz, 'Sooner or later – maybe sooner would be the best – I'm going to have to look in at Maudie Grout's place to see if he's with one of her girls. I'll tell you that now so that you'll already know it by the time it's arranged for you to overhear it in the shop.'

Liz, grinning, trying to frown at the same time, had obviously been looking about the room for something to throw at him, but by the time she found it, he had gone out, closing the door. With it her playful mood faded. Half a dozen times she had regretted her promise to Polly Marchant, days ago, and once had even been on the brink of breaking it and telling Nightgall. Now he had left once more, unknowingly, taking that particular temptation with him at least for a time.

Nightgall indeed went directly along to Maudie Grout's and although the pasty-faced girl who came part-way down the stairs, craning her neck to his calling, did not really want to go back up and wake Maudie herself, Nightgall loudly insisted, and when Maudie herself appeared, was waiting there in the garish lobby of the Wheeler, his boots planted apart and his arms folded, as though striking some premeditated attitude of defiance lest anybody question his being in there.

Maudie had on her silk wrap and her mousy hair was still wildly loose.

'I wouldn't come down at this hour for nobody else in this town, Marshal.'

'I know that Maudie, and I thank you.'

'I've got this feelin',' said Maudie, appraising him, 'that by the cut of you, you're about to ask me some damn' questions I can't answer or that I don't want to hear.'

'I'm lookin' for a man named Tyler,' Nightgall said.

She flapped a limp hand across in front of her face.

'Christ Mr Nightgall, we don't ask 'em their names! For one thing, even if we wanted to, we ain't got the time, nor them neither. For another, most of 'em from around here for reasons that you an' me can work out for ourselves, they ain't goin' to give us their right ones anyway.'

'Let me ask it a different way then,' said Nightgall. 'This Tyler, since he arrived in Wheeler has spent some time in Corrado's. He's a tall, thin man, dark, with a pocked face, an' a mean-tempered bastard. A pale, kind of sallow skin, he's got.'

Somebody else looked questioningly over a bannister, a young, freckled girl with richly red hair.

'Go on back up there Annie,' Maudie said. 'It's nobody for you.' The freckled face grinned and the girl vanished. Maudie shook her head, her attention coming back to Nightgall. 'Can't place that one by what you've said, an' I get to see 'em all that comes in. If he's gone to ground maybe he's shut in all snug with one o' Corrado's women.'

'Maybe,' Nightgall said. 'Wherever he is he's dropped from sight real sudden and I want him where I can see him.'

Her small, intelligent brown eyes were fixed on

him. My God but he was a fine strapping man though one that clearly had been hard used; but he was a good man, a fair one too, was Nightgall; a fine, rugged, handsome man. Maudie Grout would have gladly and with great alacrity bedded him simply for the pleasure of it and to assuage her curiosity, but he had his own woman, always the same one, so one way and another *she* must be something Maudie thought, really something, that Liz whatever-her-name-was. If he could read her expression he gave no sign. Ah well.

'I can't help you Mr Nightgall,' she said.

'If he does come here,' said Nightgall, 'will you say?'

She looked into space and drew a long breath, her splendidly ample bosom swelling even more under her wrap, revealing its prominent details.

'Now you're askin' somethin'. Now you really are askin' somethin'. You know what the usual thing is in a place like this. No names, no faces, no questions; nothin' but what they come in for.'

'I know,' said Nightgall, 'and I respect that Maudie, but if it wasn't important, and today in particular, I wouldn't be down here gettin' you from your bed an' asking.'

She nodded and although she was by no means dismissive, had indeed come from her bed and could not stifle a wide yawn.

'Yeah. Well, I've heard what you've said. I'll have to think about it Marshal, if it should come to pass. I'd have to think. Maybe you'll hear, maybe not. I have to go careful.' Because it was Nightgall she had a mind to give way, some, but a whore with a mouth got known, sooner or later.

'That's good enough. Thank you, Maudie. Again, I'm sorry to have got you up.'

She shrugged, then abruptly and, he could see, with a degree of mischief, she said, 'She know you've come?'

'She knows.'

'My but you're a damn' shrewd an' cautious man, Marshal.'

He gave her the faintest of faint smiles, nodded, touched the brim of his hat and left the hotel. He had believed her, that Tyler had not been there. He was of the firm opinion that if it had been possible for him to line up all the inhabitants of Wheeler, men, women and children, from the chairman of the Town Committee down to the youngest of the children at the schoolhouse, and demand of them the absolute truth about whatever he chose to ask, he would be disposed to take Maudie Grout's word before anybody else's. It was as he had often conjectured, a strange world, often far from what it seemed to be on the surface.

Among other places he went to Gollin's, looking and asking, this time for Tyler, and of course he seriously alarmed Gollin in the process. He then visited each of the Main Street saloons, leaving Corrado's until the last, but for all his quizzing there was still no sign or word of Tyler and everyone that he spoke to denied having seen the man for many days or at all. At the Silver Cat, Corrado himself, busy with early trade, had not been particularly pleased to see Nightgall, and though complaining about it, had then conducted him on a tour all through the building, both floors, finally with a triumphant, if irritated air of 'there-you-are-see-for-yourself.' Nightgall, speaking quietly, had thanked him politely and gone unhurriedly on his way, the separate, malevolent, calculating eyes of Ash Dobrey biding his good time, of Court, always watchful and wary of the big marshal, and of puffy-faced Polly Marchant, all boring into his long back as he pushed through the batwings of Corrado's, out on to Main. Polly thought, there he goes, maybe on his way back to *her*. Well, good luck there, marshal, for Mister Dobrey's sure enough gonna find he's worn out *his* welcome, anyway. She won't want to give him the time of day no more.

Corrado, going awkwardly through the crowd of noisy drinkers in a long room that was already misty with smoke, moved his head slightly, his sweat-slick face turned towards Dobrey and when the slim, neatly-attired man got up and came working his way to him, Corrado, as best he could, drew him away from the crowd and said, 'He's dead set on findin' that Tyler. You know where he is?'

'No,' said Dobrey, 'and I told him so. And I don't much care where Tyler is. Tyler's not an iron that

I've got in the fire.' Hard-eyed, the swarthy man stared at him a moment, then Dobrey, obviously dismissing Nightgall, said, 'I might go out for a while, later. This damn' place is beginning to choke a man.'

Corrado wiped a blue bandanna over his face.

'Yuh'll hear me coughin' later,' he said, 'while I'm out back countin' the takin's.'

Having checked at the livery near Gollin's Trading, Nightgall now walked into the sharp-smelling dimness of the Wheeler Livery, the one at the top end of Main, to speak to a weed of a man in there named Simms and to ask him about Tyler, and for the first time that morning he gained some information about him, for what it was worth.

'Yeah, that *hombre* had a mount in here up 'til a couple o' days back,' Simms told him. 'A strong, good lookin' chestnut it was. Come, paid up an' took the hoss away he did.'

'What time of day?'

'Time? After sundown, a bit.'

'Did he say anything while he was here? Anything to do with where he might be headed?'

'Nope. Surly bastard he was. Seen him in Corrado's a couple o' times so I recollect. Heard in there that his name was Tyler. But he didn't give *me* no name.'

'Did he have a bedroll with him?'

'He'd left that here when he come. Saddle, bedroll. He tied the bedroll on, yeah, like he was pullin' out for the trail.'

Nightgall thought about it, relieved at least to have heard something, but still uneasy.

'A rifle. Did he have a rifle?'

Simms shook his head, scratching slowly under one armpit.

'Fetched his warbag along an' a canteen, saddled up, paid me an' lit out. That's all I kin tell yuh.'

'I'm obliged to you,' said Nightgall.

The time was now 11.32 a.m. and Main had become a very busy place. Going on down near the Wheeler bank he met Asherton, on his way in, having been out attending to some matter to do with the festivities.

'Good to see you, Mr Nightgall.'

'I'll make no pretence about it, I'll be best pleased when all this is over an' done with,' Nightgall said. 'I took a walk around the back of the bank yesterday to have a good look. The yard door, is it kept locked?'

'No. No, because of the privies in the yard. The door has to be left unlocked because not everybody here has a key. But just inside, there's a side room where one of my senior clerks is at a desk nearly all day. From there he can see everybody that goes by, to and from the back door.'

Nightgall nodded. 'The man, Tyler, I told you about, seems to have gone. Simms says he took his horse and all his rig a couple of nights back.'

Asherton looked thoughtful and not a little uncomfortable.

'We should have arranged to give you some help, Mr Nightgall, while the town's filled with visitors like this. But if it's any consolation to you, I believe that once they've all seen the first train actually arrive and heard the speeches and got their celebrating over and done, Wheeler will empty out and quieten down again fairly quickly.'

'Yes,' said Nightgall, 'you're likely right, Mr Asherton.' He parted company with Asherton. He went pacing along the boardwalk in dappled sunlight, nodding, touching the brim of his hat to those people that he recognized, receiving the often curious stares of strangers he passed, aware that in his white shirt and black string tie, shallow black hat, dark pants and leather vest with the worn, dull star on it, and his watch-chain strung and the great pistol thonged to his right leg, probably he looked to them all that a marshal should be, hard and leather-skinned, neither friendly nor unfriendly, but not a man to cross.

'So that's him,' some said after he had gone by. 'That's Nightgall. Christ, he's a big bastard.'

People; a great many people there were in Wheeler on that fine morning, most with smiling, bright faces, with noisy, skipping children, on this special day out of the dull and dusty and back-aching routine of their lives, all come to Wheeler to watch the first train come in. Yet in spite of it all, the bustle and laughter, the festival atmosphere under the bunting, Nightgall could not rid himself of the strange apprehension that had settled on him. He had been perfectly sincere when he had remarked to Asherton that he would be best pleased when it was all over and done with.

SIX

Nightgall had looked in on Liz but she had been fully occupied attending to customers and had not even noticed that he had been there, hovering near the doorway, so he had gone across to his own place and once there made coffee and then walked through into the office at the front, and now stood sipping the scalding drink and staring through the large, grimy window on to Main. He tried to put aside the fact that from time to time his head ached dully and his knee still pained him. It was a time to gather himself, try to clear his mind and prepare himself to emerge again, see and be seen, present to the town an appearance of easy normality. Especially for Liz. Whatever happened – if anything happened – it would be his problem, not hers. He must take good care not to burden her. With an effort he cleared his mind of all that and began to concentrate on what he saw as immediate concerns.

Across the street stood a general store and next to it one of the town liveries. Back the other way, to his left, was the shadowed cut of an alley, separating the store from the shop where Liz was, then a freight office and then the bank. Beyond that, across another alley was Gollin's Trading Company, the Wheeler Hotel, then the feed and grain.

From where he stood, from that angle, he could view only as far as the bank's doorway; in any case it was only the bank that he was concerned about. For what must have been the tenth time in recent days he mulled it all over and then put to himself the questions which seemed to him to be crucial and to which he now urgently needed answers. Either that or he really was getting too old for it and he had got bloody Tyler fixed in his mind so firmly that he could not see past him.

If there is to be an attempt on the bank, when is it likely to be?

It was patently obvious: while still flush with funds from Wheeler's business boom: therefore today.

If Asherton has money moved from the bank to the secure railroad van, what precautions will he take?

A reserved man but a precise one, he will consult with the marshal nearer to the time, require his reassuring presence at the transfer and he might also have on hand the promised railroad guards and maybe even a few of the Town Committee, also, unhappily, armed, to not much more purpose than a show of additional strength.

What then will be the best time for any attempt on the bank's money?

Before the transfer to the train.

But Tyler has gone, has he not?

Tyler has paid a visit to one of the liveries and has taken his horse away. That's all.

If Tyler should return, perhaps in the company of associates who had perhaps been holed-up somewhere outside of town, when would he come?

Between now and 1 p.m. when they say the train is due. During the next hour and a quarter.

What will Tyler see as the best possible time?

Perhaps when the train is first sighted, when all attention is drawn to it, when there is high excitement.

Nightgall quietly finished his coffee. He had considered, as his best course, walking over to the bank and establishing himself in plain sight on the bench outside it, trusting that his very presence might be sufficient to deter Tyler if indeed he did come back, but almost at once he had rejected the notion. For one thing it was probable that it would not influence a man like Tyler in the slightest, particularly if he had some other hard boys along with him; for another, Nightgall himself was a restlessly energetic man when under any kind of tension and did not really fancy passing more than an hour of his time sitting on a bench outside the Wheeler bank or anywhere else. And yet another worrying aspect of this particular day was that there were so many folk on Main and around Wheeler generally, so that if the worst did happen and it came to violence there were plenty of people who could get caught up in it and be put at grave risk as well as hampering his own movements. He carried his empty coffee mug down past the stale cells back into the kitchen and rinsed it clean, then picked up his hat and went out through the front door, locking it behind him.

Nightgall went pacing around some of the back streets, very watchful, took a look at the railroad depot that smelled strongly of new wood and where a growing crowd was assembling, some shading their eyes against the hazy glare of distance, children running and skipping here and there and one or two young riders going racing away on their ponies alongside the shiny tracks for a matter of a few hundred yards, perhaps hoping to be the first ones in Wheeler to glimpse the smoke from the very first train. Well, if it was running to time, they were a mite early for that, thought Nightgall. He returned to Main and walked slowly along the boardwalk on the opposite side of the street from the bank. Ash Dobrey, standing just inside the batwing doors of Corrado's place stared dourly at the marshal's back and waited until he had got well away before emerging, grey hat now on his head, immaculate in the pre-noon, stepping across the dusty street like some fastidious water bird. At first, Gollin, seeing him, thought he was heading towards the

Trading Company, but Dobrey merely offered him a casual wave and went inside the telegraph office. The message he sought had come in hours earlier but had been left aside in the excitement.

Nightgall plodded on. Twice he paused to speak with townsfolk, then he crossed over Main diagonally going down towards Liz's place. It was at that instant, when he glanced along that way, that he caught sight of Tyler, far down Main near the Simms livery, and on foot. Though other people were criss-crossing Main and passing buggies and then a buckboard were raising dust and the distance between them was reasonably long, Nightgall saw him and knew even as he did so that Tyler had seen him, and it was as though the street was empty. Careless of moving wheels, Nightgall immediately began to jog-trot along the middle of Main, keeping his eyes fixed firmly on Tyler who now, seemingly in some alarm, as though caught out in some felony, was seeking to get himself out of sight again. A number of people saw the big marshal running, a little girl pointed, others stopped and turned to look but Nightgall ran on, apparently oblivious to all of them, wheel-dust enveloping him at one moment, reappearing in the clear the next. He reached the big open doorway of the livery, breathing short, but he was too late, Tyler had gone. Nightgall, mindful of a mistake he had made in the recent past, drew the long pistol and as soon as passers-by saw the glint of that in the bright sun, there was near panic in that part of the street and a hurried backing off. Women herded their children away.

Nightgall shouted towards the livery, 'Simms!'

The weedy little man appeared hesitantly in the shadowed doorway. He knew what Nightgall was there for.

'Gone on through.'

Nightgall swore softly. If Tyler had got to a horse then he was away again and Nightgall himself was no further advanced except that he now knew for certain that Tyler was still in the vicinity and wanted no truck with the town marshal. Nightgall trotted on anyway, through the rich-smelling dimness of the place, horses in the stalls moving and blowing on either side of him, straw making rushing sounds under his feet, until he came into brightness again, and the corral yard out back. Again he suddenly saw Tyler, over near a barn just beyond the corral and called to him, but once again the man dodged very quickly from sight. Now Nightgall was more wary than ever, going along slowly, remembering events near a barn at the opposite end of Wheeler, when he had been heading after Stokes and when it turned out that Stokes, in spite of the way it had looked, had merely been drawing him on for other purposes. Nightgall stopped. Several horses inside the livery corral had raised their heads and were evaluating him. Dry planks on the back wall of the livery ticked desolately in the heat.

Nightgall, after his efforts, was sweating freely and some of the dust that had been raised on Main was clinging to his skin and his clothing. The big pistol was held, right arm crooked, the butt of it about the level of his right ear, long barrel pointing straight upwards, the great solid weight of the thing in his large hand. For a few seconds he stood unmoving trying to make up his mind on the best course to take.

Word had travelled quite quickly among the many people on Main and even in her busy shop, Liz had become aware of some sort of excitement outside. It was not until she thought she caught the word *marshal* though, that she hastily finished attending to a customer, and in a temporary lull, went out herself on to the boardwalk. Anxiously she glanced first one way then the other but was unable to see any sign at all of Nightgall, but with the large number of folk about on Main, it was difficult, anyway, to tell exactly who was there. Some small groups, though standing well away, seemed to be staring up beyond her towards the livery. A small boy went trotting by, heading towards the insistent calling of his mother, but had time to look at Liz, his eyes shining.

'The marshal runned! The marshal runned with a gun!'

Liz felt cold dread clutch at her and for a moment felt unsteady and had to put one of her slim hands against a veranda post. When a young man from Torrens' General Store came hurrying by, his white apron flapping she asked, 'Do you know what's going on?'

The lad wanted urgently to go on, but as it was Liz, paused, but was shaking his head.

'I didn't actually *see* nothin' myself, Miz Ellwood, but they do say that Mr Nightgall come runnin' hell-bent right up Main with his pistol drawn, come runnin' all through the buggies an' horses an' all, not sayin' nothin' until he shouted out to Simms down there an' then went on into the livery.'

She nodded. 'Thank you.' The boy went hurrying away.

However there was still no sign whatsoever of Nightgall but at least the one good thing was that there had been no gunfire. She wondered if it could have been the man Tyler that he had been running after so determinedly, and what might have happened to make Tyler want to run, anyway. It was at just such times as these that she felt defenceless and impotent, yet partly angry at the same time, as though she was almost resenting the hold that this man's presence, his being, exercised over her, when once long ago, she had sworn to herself that whatever happened, no other would ever have such a claim on her life. And commonly it was after such frightening events as these that upon next seeing Nightgall, sometimes she found she could not help venting this anger upon him, although she always knew full well that she was doing so quite unfairly; but she also knew, and she believed that he realized that it was a real fear for him, for his welfare, that fuelled it, fear and other, much deeper and less often admitted emotions. When she straightened and took her hand from the dry wooden post she could feel a dampness in her palm.

Little by little the movements up and down Main were returning to normal. Nothing more had happened. There was nothing to see. There had been no sounds. Liz herself had turned to go back into the shop when suddenly and with some surprise she saw that Ash Dobrey had come along the boardwalk unnoticed, and raising his grey hat elegantly, with a certain flourish, now stood before her.

'I heard there was some kind of trouble, Miz Ellwood, somewhere along here, and I felt concerned. Are you all right?'

'Of course,' she said. 'There's no trouble here, as you can well see.'

This was not the calm and pleasant woman with whom he had sometimes passed the time of day and who occupied his mind much more than ever she could have imagined. And while she had never in the least encouraged him, had done nothing to reject him, either. Yet now, unexpectedly, there was a tautness in her tone, almost a brusqueness in the way that she had spoken to him, and though he did not visibly react and continued to look at her with a neutral expression, this cold reception had taken him aback. Perhaps, he thought defensively, it was simply that, because of something that had happened, she had been badly shaken. He decided that the best way to respond was to speak calmly and quietly, as though her attitude had not even been noticed.

'There are so many new people here in town now,' he said, 'all kinds of people, unfortunately, that we all have to take more care.'

'I am perfectly capable of taking good care of myself, Mr Dobrey, never fear. You have no call to concern yourself at all on my behalf.'

Quite definitely, while she had spoken without particular emphasis, she was on the very brink of rudeness towards him and try though he might, he could not even imagine why it should be so. At their previous casual meeting she had been cordial enough, chatting easily; very correct in her manner, to be sure, but yes, cordial. But her present tone seemed out of keeping with what he had perceived to be her very nature.

'But I do fear,' said Dobrey boldly, thinking to test her, 'and I do care what might happen to you. That's why I'm here.'

Colour had flushed into her face now.

'Then you have absolutely no need to do so,' she said, 'for I have all the protection that any woman anywhere could possibly wish for, Mr Dobrey, from Marshal Nightgall himself.' Indeed she was angry now. 'You must be well aware, surely, that Nightgall *lives* with me, or as near to it as makes no difference. Yes surely you do, for I'm certain that everyone else here in Wheeler knows it, and some of them even take it upon themselves to resent it or to disapprove of it, or whatever you want to call it. But I feel secure with Nightgall, safe; safe from all of the predators that there are, even at the best of times, and safe *with* him, for hard man that he surely is, he knows how to treat a woman.' And with deep anger and hurt driving her, she could not prevent herself from adding, 'And he is a man who would never, even in the wildest of his wild moods, sink to *mistreating* a woman.'

Dobrey stood before her with his face drained of colour, his mind reeling under what he knew now was intended as an outright personal attack. It had not been fear at all that today had caused her to be abrasive with him right from the start. It had been scorn, distaste, dislike and perhaps even much more than that; and she had gone out of her way to rub his nose in the fact of Nightgall's eternal presence. His mouth set firm, still ashen-faced he merely touched the brim of his hat and turned and walked away.

Now Liz, standing there watching him go soon to be lost among others, began to think over in a calmer frame of mind exactly what she had said to him and wondered numbly if, in venting her sharp anger, she had in fact gone too far, and had witlessly compromised poor Polly Marchant. Nightgall's words came suddenly back to her with ringing clarity:

'*...don't you spit in Dobrey's eye for the sake of it.*

Don't be taken in by that smile he puts on … be polite … he's a hard man is Dobrey.' Perhaps now she might simply *have* to say something to Nightgall. She turned her head to look towards the livery. Of Nightgall there was still no sign at all. She went back inside the shop, for other customers had now arrived.

A door opened and closed softly and when Asherton's back-room clerk glanced up from the work on his desk, Gates, the albino, was there, his thonged, greasy old hat hanging between his sharp shoulder blades, his strange short white hair startlingly apparent and his unbelievable, pinkish eyes burning from his pale face with insane fires. He, this unnatural apparition in ragged clothes, was the last living thing on earth that the bank clerk saw as he half-rose from his chair, for the long barrel of Gates' pistol, whipping in a swift, glittering arc, smashed hard against his right temple, a blow so savage that a splinter of bone was driven deep into his brain. The clerk went crashing over his chair to the bare floor and lay there, half against the far wall, blood beginning to ooze from his head, short, soft snorting noises coming from him. Gates paused, his body half-turned towards the still-open door, his whole frame tense as he stood listening. He remained thus for very nearly the span of one minute before relaxing. There were no voices, no pounding of feet. Apparently nobody had heard the man and the chair go down. Gates slid the big pistol back into its holster. For a brief time he assessed the situation, then, stooping, he seized the fallen man by the front of the shirt and with a degree of awkwardness dragged him around into a position behind the desk, in which place he might less easily be seen by anyone going by in the passageway. He then picked up the chair and stood it on its legs. So, the first part of it was now accomplished. He was in.

Inside his own office near the front of the building Asherton glanced at the clock that was attached to the far wall: 11.55 a.m.. In about five minutes time some of his people would leave to take their meal break. When that happened, he himself would go out into the general banking area, and though he might not be needed, would if necessary lend a hand, for there would be only one clerk remaining out there, the other, and the young woman having left.

Already he had supervised the filling of several canvas bags in the strongroom and had personally prepared all necessary documents needed for shipment of the excess money up to the bigger bank at Coleman. Earlier that morning, the telegraph had been sent out about it. When the currency arrived at Coleman, additional security in the shape of deputies would be waiting at the depot there. More than once, however, since talking with Nightgall, Asherton had wished that he had taken the initiative and insisted upon temporary deputies being sworn in here in

Wheeler, to serve at least until such time as the train had departed once again. That particular matter had not been in any way up to Nightgall, whose authority to deputize was clearly restricted by the Wheeler Town Committee, to the formation of a posse in exceptional circumstances, say after a felony had occurred. After the horse has bolted, thought Asherton, not without chagrin, for he knew that the responsibility was chiefly his own. Under all other circumstances, it had been made plain that deputies might only be appointed at the discretion of the Town Committee. The reason was purely mercenary; deputies could be costly. Asherton drummed his fingers on his desk and looked at the clock again and saw that it was but a few seconds short of noon. The manager of the Wheeler bank stood up.

Nightgall had made a slow, most careful circuit of the barn before entering it by a side door that he found and making a thorough search of it, but it had been to no avail. There was really no place else to look. He had lost Tyler. Disconsolately he returned to the livery and spoke again to the man Simms, who told him that he had not set eyes on Tyler since he had seen him run through the place, earlier.

'An' I got out the front way real fast,' he admitted, 'for I kin tell yuh I shore didn't fancy the looks o' that feller nohow, Marshal.'

Nightgall, moving at last back on to Main was

puzzled, for he had received the impression that, even as Stokes had done, though perhaps not quite as blatantly, Tyler had shown himself deliberately, otherwise why would he have come out on to the street at all, and on foot? Or maybe the plan, if Tyler had had one, had changed; maybe the bank itself was no longer the target, though Nightgall was inclined to think that it was. There were, however, places between Wheeler and Coleman at which the train might be brought to a halt by a bunch of road agents who were determined enough, and then, secure and guarded van or not, there would be a limit to how long such a group of men could be held off. On the boardwalk outside Liz Ellwood's shop he glanced in and touched his hat as he went by, suddenly wanting her to know that, whatever she might have heard to the contrary, he was so far unharmed. He thumbed his watch out and looked at it. 12.15 p.m. In a little more than half an hour they could expect to sight the smoke from the locomotive and even now, more of the people were tending to drift towards the far end of the town, and a good-sized crowd had begun to form a ragged line between the depot and the water tower, the latter now filled, though dripping from new seams, and with its canvas hose hanging in readiness. Nightgall spoke to a man wearing a green eyeshade; this was Forbes of the stage-line office, a pot-bellied man in a striped grey shirt and wide galluses.

'Bad day for you, Gus?'

'Naw, not all that bad, Marshal. This here stage line is gonna be here a good while yet. There's plenty places the railroad won't go through for some long time, I reckon. We won't be asked to carry a strongbox near as often, o' course, but I cain't say that I'm bleedin' a lot about that.' Forbes once, and for some years, a stage-line guard, would walk all of his life with a slight limp, from an attempt on a stage, by bandits, years ago. Forbes, unlikely as it might have seemed to any who did not know him well, had had his moments.

'Do something for me Gus?'

'Name it.' If there was anybody at all in Wheeler whom the laconic, bluff stage-line man could be said to respect above anybody else there, it was this man Nightgall. They had, in their distinct and separate ways, looked into the black-eyed barrel and had been through the gunsmoke, and it made the difference.

'You know Liz Ellwood well enough.'

'That I do.'

'There are some here in Wheeler that she'd not welcome in her place, Gus, but you don't happen to be one of 'em. If there should be any problems here today, any sort of trouble, will you take your shotgun and go right away down to the shop and kind of watch out for her?'

'Right quick I will,' said Forbes. He hooked his broad, broken-nailed thumbs in his galluses and waited until a small group of people had passed by before, squinting now at the big man, he asked, 'What kind o' problems in partic'lar?'

Nightgall too, with a glance, made quite sure that no one else was within earshot before he said, 'There might be a try for the bank. If there is, it might come soon. If it does happen it could happen fast, so take care if you have to go on down there with the shotgun.'

'Jesus,' Forbes said softly. 'Look, Nightgall, I kin go load up right now an' present my own damn' problem from this here doorway.'

'No, no, Gus. I'm the only man in Wheeler who gets paid for doin' that. I knew damn' well that you'd offer to do it, but don't put yourself at risk. Will you give me that assurance?'

Forbes shrugged. If that was what Nightgall wanted.

'As yuh'll have it, then. Come any shootin' I'll git on down to that shop.' But he couldn't help but look shrewdly at Nightgall. 'If yuh figure she might be in need of a friendly eye, then yuh must have some good notion of who might be *unfriendly* while you was otherwise engaged.'

At first, Nightgall thought he would not show his hand even to Forbes but knew that in all fairness he had little option in view of the considerable favour he was asking of the man. And there was another thing and it needed to be faced: if he himself went down, Liz had no one.

'There's people around, some of 'em up at Corrado's, that are not well disposed to me,' he said. 'They might see it as a God-sent chance to … to reach me.'

Forbes stood looking at him silently for a moment or two, then he nodded.

'Understood.'

'I'm obliged,' said Nightgall, and moved on.

At the top-end livery, Simms had had enough excitement for one day and had decided to stroll to the opposite end of town and like everybody else, get himself a look at the approach of the train from Coleman, an event which ought to be taking place quite soon by all the estimates.

As soon as he had departed there came a faint stirring in the rafters in the upper gloom of the building, and presently Tyler, hanging first by his gloved hands, let go and struck and rolled in thick straw, then got up, brushing it from his clothing, and went out the back door of the livery.

They had been arguing again, this time seriously. Dobrey had heard the hard-hissed whispers between them in the upper passageway, had heard Court go into a room and slam the door and now met Polly Marchant on the landing.

'A word with you, Polly.'

One hand came up to her mouth for he had startled her, but then a faint flush stole into her face.

'Yes?' *God, did he know*?

Surprisingly, he reached out and took her hand away from her face, but quite gently, and he remained holding her fingers a moment before releasing them.

'They say you're really too good for the bastard, Polly.'

She could not believe that it was Ash Dobrey who was saying this to her. Ash Dobrey. Here, on this landing with her. He was standing very close indeed, looking down at her, speaking softly. Yet she had to say, 'I have to go – to get down there.' But she was vastly relieved. He did not know. He could not know that she had spoken to Liz Ellwood about *him*.

'They can wait,' Dobrey said. The odd thing was that he had never bothered to speak to her this way before. On the contrary, he had been much more remote. She had even thought sometimes, that he actually despised her; but now, suddenly here he was, alone with her, and by his own wish.

'I overheard,' he said, 'and I heard Bill go back in and slam the door.'

She looked down, away from him, suddenly embarrassed.

'Sometimes we ... don't get along.'

'I know,' said Dobrey in the same low voice. 'A man would have to be blind not to see it.' With much gentleness he touched the side of her silky face. 'You've been hurt, Polly. Don't look startled. I saw, after it must have happened, that you'd been hurt.' One of his fingers touched her lower lip where the cut was. 'Did he do that?' She looked away again, not wanting to answer him, shrinking from the shame of it. And what if Court should come out of the room and come to the stairs? 'Did he do that?'

'Please don't ... don't ask him... about that.'

'Polly? He did that?' There was no avoiding it. She nodded her head jerkily, holding back tears. 'Did he hurt you any other way?'

One of her hands moved vaguely to indicate an upper arm.

'There are ... some bruises.'

'So he does beat you?'

'Not ... often. Sometimes, when he's been drinking. Don't all men ...?' She choked it off.

Dobrey continued to look down at her, then gently took her chin and tilted her face so that she could not avoid looking at him.

'Not all men,' said Dobrey quietly. 'Not by any means. Men like Bill Court, maybe. Polly, you went along and you talked with Liz Ellwood about being hurt.'

Her eyes dilated slightly.

'I—'

'You told Liz Ellwood about it, Polly. You went down there to her shop with only that on your mind, to tell her.' His voice was still quite soft but there was no warmth in it now. There was another, a strange quality there and it alarmed her. 'You allowed her to believe, Polly, that *I* was the man who'd hurt you.'

'No!'

'Oh yes. It couldn't have been any other way.

Why? Why did you use my name and lie to her?'

Tears came, bright on her pale cheeks. She shook her head.

'Please ...!'

'You lied Polly, deliberately, and there's no use at all your denying that you did. That being so, what you will do, this very day, without fail, is go back up there to that shop and talk again with Liz Ellwood, and you will explain to her that you lied, that it was Court who did that to you, and that I have never, never been near you. After you've done that, and absolutely convinced her, you will never go near Liz Ellwood again for as long as you remain here in Wheeler. Not ever. You must remember your place, Polly, remember who *she* is and remember who *you* are. One day, though you choose not to believe it, Liz Ellwood will be *my* woman, while you Polly, you are and always will be, a tenth-rate bar-dog's slut. Fail to do what I've told you to do, and I promise that quite soon, a half-dozen of Corrado's bigger and dirtier men will take you up to a room at Frater's and when they've done with you, Polly, I promise you that a *real* dog would sniff you and walk away.'

Abruptly he turned and left her.

The clerk's name was Peters and when Asherton walked through to join him there were only a couple of customers remaining, and he thought that probably business would remain relatively quiet now until the excitement of the first train was over. Main for sure had fewer people on it, even the railroad gangers themselves and many of the folk who had been professing disinterest having at last succumbed to curiosity. When the two customers in the bank had been dealt with, Asherton said, 'When the others come back at 12.30 I have to go across to meet the train. I don't know how long I'll be over there.'

Peters nodded. 'I understand, Mr Asherton.'

'Where is Gilby? Gone with the others?'

'I've not actually seen Gil since earlier this morning sir. If he's gone out, I guess maybe he left by the back door.'

Asherton rubbed at his jaw.

'If he has,' he said, 'I hope he's taken the precaution of locking it. I told him to do that any time he was not going to be right at his desk back there. I must just go check on that.'

'Yuh won't do nothin', banker,' Gates said. The albino was there, had seemingly come out of nowhere, standing in his dirty old clothes, and smelling like an animal, his abominable hat hanging at his back by its thongs, the awful black eye of the great pistol he held in his right hand looking frighteningly large and full of menace. Shocked, Peters moved instinctively to back away but Gates squinted at him and shifted the pistol slightly and in his oddly nasal voice said, 'Yuh move ag'in, boy, an' they'll have to scrape up yore asshole off of Main.' Peters stood stock still.

Now that the first pulsing shock of the albino's

arrival was past, Asherton asked, 'How did you get in? Where is Gilby?'

'If he's that bastard out back don't yuh be in a all-fired rush to go look. *He* shore ain't goin' no place, 'cept when an' where the devil hisself tells him.'

'If he's been harmed ...' Asherton began.

'If he's been harmed – what? What, banker? If he's been harmed, what? Now you jes' shut yore prissy hole or I'll let yuh have a bite on this.' Again he moved the pistol so that the barrel wagged. 'Go git the money out. I know there's plenty here. You,' – moving his white-haired head at Peters – 'you help him.'

Peters, his face colourless but shiny with sweat, looked at Asherton, who nodded.

'We'll do as he says. We can't argue with the pistol.'

There came a slight, unaccountable noise. The albino suddenly backed away two paces and glanced quickly through the doorway that led to the back of the building.

''Bout time.'

Tyler came sauntering in as though there was all the time in the world.

'I've jes' told 'em to go git the money,' Gates said.

'Then why ain't they doin' it?' Tyler turned his badly pocked, shiny face towards Asherton. 'I'd do it quick was I you, banker.'

Asherton, trailed by the clerk, Peters, moved along slowly behind the tellers' counter towards the strongroom which, once the cash drawers had been set up at the beginning of the day, had been closed at Asherton's instructions, and locked.

'Open it,' Tyler said, 'by the time I count to three or I'll shoot the balls off'n Homer, here.'

Asherton did not hesitate but set to at once and opened the sturdy door. Meantime the albino walked around the counter and over to the Main Street door, closed and locked it, sliding bolts across, and then at the nearby window, drew down the blind. He came walking back, spurs clinking. By this time they were carrying the canvas sacks out of the strongroom.

'Twine,' Tyler was saying, 'where's some goddamn' twine, Homer?'

Peters knew he meant him, and was scrabbling around looking, fruitlessly it seemed at first, until he discovered some under one of the counters.

'Cut some lengths of that,' said Tyler. 'Make a neck on each sack. Double up the twine for strength an' tie the sacks together in pairs, an' make damn' sure the twine's long enough to go across the horse.' Peters, though fumbling in his anxiety and haste, was getting on with it.

'Now this,' the albino said, 'is what I *call* a bank hold-up. It's got some class. Ain't no shoutin' an' ain't no runnin' an' ain't no shootin' off o' the pistols. What we got here is a civilized thing. Yes sir. Not like down there in San Christo where there wuz all that bangin' an' screamin' an' carryin' on.'

Faintly, over distance, like some prolonged and

plaintive cry, came the sound of a train whistle.

'Very soon,' said Asherton, afraid but controlling his voice well, 'someone will come looking for me because of the train.'

'Ho, will they now?' the albino said, his pinkish eyes staring wide. 'Will they now. Well, won't that be a case?' He made his voice an uncanny mimicry of Asherton's voice. 'I cain't come over there right off, friends, 'cos I'm occupied at the bank, supervisin' gittin' cleaned out or raped or whatever. But don't yuh worry none friends, fer it's got real class,' and they doubled up, laughing, him and Tyler, both. Then abruptly they stopped laughing and there was a dangerous silence.

Tyler said, 'Come on then yuh bastards, move yore fat asses an' carry them sacks out back.'

Asherton and Peters, taking two bags apiece, hefted them and went out along the passageway towards the back of the bank, Tyler and Gates following closely.

They had got four of the bags up and slung on the light-hitched horses, the twine doubled around the saddle horns, and they were coming back in for more when a noise came from the front door of the bank.

Nightgall had taken a good look at the considerable crowd now waiting for the train and when someone said that they could see something, he along with others shaded his eyes, looking far down the line of the gleaming rails, but it was impossible as yet to determine whether or not it was smoke that had been seen. Again, the crowd, having stirred, settled back to wait, many of them now sitting under roughly rigged-up awnings, seeking some relief from the burning sun.

Nightgall could see that the whole town itself was quieter, partly from the heat, partly from the waiting, but thought that nonetheless he would maybe take another stroll along the boardwalk on one side of Main. Something else had occurred to him. He did think that it was odd that he had not noticed Asherton up there along with other members of the Town Committee who had been standing in a separate group at the depot itself. He walked on. The bank stood on the side of the street opposite from where he now was, and as he came abreast of the place, stopped and looked at it with close interest. At no earlier time had Asherton mentioned that he might actually close the bank. All he had said was that when the guards from the special railroad van arrived, the money would be taken across to the train in canvas sacks and he would at that stage appreciate Nightgall's being on hand. But now quite clearly the front door of the place was closed and the window blind had been drawn down. Nightgall, out of curiosity, began to walk slowly across the street in the direction of the bank. Very few people were about but he had noticed a brightly-dressed woman going along towards the farther end of Main and at that glance thought that there had been something familiar about her. But his attention was now diverted by the sight of the watchful Gus Forbes standing in the doorway of the stage-line office, looking towards him, apparently sensing, with the keenness of a man who had himself faced grave risks, that Nightgall's attention had been seized by something unusual. Two yards short of the boardwalk near to the bank, Nightgall paused, and in a low voice, just loud enough to carry to Forbes, he said, 'Asherton?' The question and its implication was picked up immediately by the man in the doorway, who shrugged and then shook his head. No, he had not seen the man in recent hours.

Nightgall mounted the boardwalk and stood looking carefully at the door, then at the window with its drawn blind. A precaution perhaps, on Asherton's part now that business had probably fallen away, while awaiting the train? Though possible, somehow Nightgall doubted it. Asherton was a calm and quite precise man. It would have been more in keeping with his style to have told Nightgall in detail what he intended doing, certainly told him of any change in plans; and surely he would have taken care to keep the other members of his Town Committee informed. Nightgall glanced again towards Forbes who had got hold of his double-barrelled shotgun and because the marshal had now come to the firm belief that something might indeed be wrong, motioned abruptly to Forbes who at once went limping off in the direction of the far end of Wheeler, where Liz Ellwood's shop was. Nightgall was taking no chances.

One other circumstance now loomed large in Nightgall's mind. There were no horses standing here at the hitching-rail, but that of course did not necessarily mean that there were no horses anywhere near the bank. There was always the yard.

From a long, hot distance came the unmistakable wailing of a train whistle and right after it, floating insubstantially on the heated air, a ragged cheer. It was coming.

Nightgall, however, still felt that he had to give Asherton a chance to explain what was going on and therefore hesitated for a minute or two, for the train might well have been heard from inside the bank. Forbes was now well along Main, though moving with his awkward gait, and in fact at this time, seemed to be the only other living thing abroad on the street. Finally Nightgall thought that he could delay no longer and made up his mind and strode across the boardwalk to try the door handle.

For the past few minutes Liz Ellwood had been debating with herself about simply closing up the shop so that she might go along herself to see the arrival of the train and she had just made up her mind to do so when Polly Marchant came in. Liz could see at once that the girl was badly upset, her cheeks flushed and puffy with recent tears, and because she was bare-headed, her hair was partly loose, strands of it plastered against the wetness of her face. As soon as she was inside the shop the shouting began.

'You *told* him, you bitch! You *told* him!'

'Told who?' For a moment Liz was physically set back a pace and she was confused by the sudden, the loud, immediate flaring of anger that the girl had unleashed upon her. Having already come around the end of the shop counter preparatory to closing the street door, Liz found that, involuntarily, she had backed off as far as the counter itself. Polly Marchant had stopped a matter of three feet away, her pretty face distorted with venom and her slim body leaning forward, breasts heaving beneath her yellow blouse, one hand partly extended, the other tangled in the folds of her brightly-patterned yellow, red and black skirt.

'He come here again, didn't he?' Polly shouted.

Liz, calmer now, recovering composure, saw no point in denial.

'If you mean Ash Dobrey, yes, he's been here.'

'An' you *told* him what I said!'

'Ash Dobrey came as far as the shop door while I was outside on the boardwalk. He had no need to come. I sent him away.'

'You're a liar!'

Very firmly, Liz said, '*I sent him away*. More than that, I gave him quite clearly to understand that I had no need of him and certainly I did *not* need his protection as, for some unknown reason, he seemed to think.'

'That ain't all you said to Dobrey!' shouted Polly. She had come a pace closer. 'An' I don't *believe* what you say, anyway, you lawman's whore! You turned Ash Dobrey *against* me!'

'Your name was never mentioned,' Liz told her, choosing to ignore the gross insult. 'It's true he did make me angry by his – his assumptions, and while I was angry I told him I had all the protection and all the care I would ever need, in Marshal Nightgall, a man who was not in the habit of striking women.'

'There! There, y'see? You *told* him!'

'Look,' said Liz, becoming angry herself now, 'you told me Dobrey had struck you and had bruised you. You made your own decision to tell me that. If he *didn't* do it, and if he took my remark up and guessed what you'd told me, I expect he's taken you to task about it, and I think that's why you're here, with no more marks on you. That's it, isn't it?' It was no use though.

'He'll *have* you, lady! That's what he says. Do you know that? He'll *have* you. Well, I'm here to say he won't *want* you no more when he does come for you!' Her right hand came suddenly into view as she moved forward again and Liz went cold with horror and felt her knees all but give way when the open razor glittered above her, to strike at her face. Desperately she went plunging to the side.

'Stop it! Put it away Polly!'

'Like hell I'll put it away!' Her slim arm was up and the winking wafer of honed steel was cutting down when Liz sprang forward, both hands clutching for Polly Marchant's elbow. The desperation of terror lent her speed and an unexpectedly fierce strength as her fingers closed around Polly's arm and she struggled to push it up and to the side. So in that reaching attitude they collided, gasping, tussling, the fine blade held high as they lurched and bumped this way and that, sometimes knocking against the merchandise, some racks of clothing falling over, spilling the garments in heaps. Then Liz caught her foot in something that had fallen and all at once the other woman was free of her, free with the open razor, and Liz was on her knees and she knew that this time she would not be able to evade it. Polly Marchant drew her arm back and Liz saw the glint of the awful thing as it came slicing down towards her. But when the quick fire of the thin steel should have opened up her face, there was nothing except a sharp cry bursting from Polly Marchant.

'*Let me go*!'

Forbes, of the stage-line was there, one strong hand clamped around Polly's right wrist, lifting her bodily so that her shoes barely touched the floor. In his other hand, counterbalancing, Forbes held his long shotgun. He then drew down his own arm until, her shoes clumping on the floor again, Polly's was extended at right angles to her body.

'Let the razor go, Pol,' Forbes said, though not loudly. 'Let it go.' He even shook her wrist gently and the dreadful blade fell and clattered on the floorboards.

Liz was getting to her feet, her face devoid of colour, her limbs trembling. She could not remember when she had been as frightened as she had been during the past few minutes.

But Polly Marchant was no longer a threat. The fury that had driven her suddenly was spent and she had crumpled to the floor, head hanging, hair in disarray, deep sobs racking her. In spite of herself and all that had happened, Liz went to her. Then they heard the dull sound of gunshots, as though from inside some building, and a good distance off.

Nightgall twisted again at the doorhandle but to no response. The door was indeed locked.

'Asherton! It's Nightgall!'

Again the train whistle came hauntingly, sounding much closer now. From inside the bank there was still no answer to his call. He had turned and gone a couple of paces to the left, intending to go around and down the alley to the back of the building, and it was that movement which saved him; for at that moment somewhere inside the place a heavy pistol boomed and the door itself shuddered, bursting with splinters. Another thundering shot came and window glass flew as the dark blue blind was punched through it. But Nightgall was moving fast now and was already at the corner of the building. Across the street a startled face appeared. Someone from the train crowd, running to see, and the marshal paused but only for a moment.

'Tell 'em – tell everybody to stay off Main or risk gettin' shot!' He went on then, jogging down the alley. At an upper window at Gollin's he glimpsed other faces, but whoever they were they pulled back as soon as they saw that it was the marshal, going quickly, pistol drawn, and that he had noticed them.

By the time he got around to the opening to the back yard of the bank he was breathing fire in his windpipe and he had to pause to recover himself, and just as well, for they were out in the yard now, near the horses, Tyler, Gates the albino, Asherton and the clerk, Peters. Tyler had got the bank men standing so that had Nightgall chosen to fire they would have been in the gravest danger of being the first hit. The albino was busy settling canvas sacks on either side of the horses, to his satisfaction; in such a position, Nightgall saw, that they would just about rest against both knees of a mounted man.

'Don't come no closer!' Tyler called. Nightgall did not push it and even drew back a little, where he was, at the corner of an outhouse, the sharp, penetrating stench of the privies in his nostrils, but still in a position from which he could see all of the group near the back door of the bank. 'Yuh've left it a touch late, Marshal!'

'You're not away yet,' Nightgall said, his deep voice carrying easily.

'As good as,' said Tyler. 'An' I'll give yuh one more as-good-as. One little move from yuh that looks to me like aggra-vation, an' ol' banker here, an' Homer here, they're as good as dog meat. Like, it's plenty bad enough for 'em now. Gates here, he ain't exac'ly what yuh'd call took a shine to Homer as it is.' The albino came around the heads of the horses to join Tyler just behind the other two men. Asherton obviously said something then, but the albino told him to shut up. Asherton in fact had said that he wanted Peters to be released.

'So, what's it to be then, Marshal?' Tyler asked. They heard the loud sound of a train whistle several times repeated, a sound of triumphant greeting, and people shouting and cheering over the rushing noise of the locomotive. 'What's it to be on this great day in Wheeler?'

Nightgall felt it possible that at least a few among the assembled townsfolk, out of curiosity, might soon come to find out what was really going on, but at the same time he almost prayed that they would not. Having these two bank men here, both at grave risk, was more than enough for him to be worrying about. He called, 'Let 'em go, Tyler!' He thought that eventually they would have to be let go anyway rather than be taken as hostages, for there were no other horses in the yard and Tyler could not afford to delay too long in pulling out.

'I'll let these bastards off the hook when yuh git yore face well away,' called Tyler. 'If yuh start shittin' me about, then these boys are in deep trouble. Yuh hear that? Understand that?'

'I hear it,' said Nightgall, 'but you'll not get far.'

'If yuh got ideas about the telegraph,' said Tyler, 'forget 'em. That partic'lar wire won't be singin' no songs o' the Wheeler bank, not fer a while. Gates here's 'tended to that already. An' a good long stretch o' that wire ain't gonna be found no more.' Nightgall's eyes narrowed. The telegraph was something he should have thought about. What with the first news of the train, earlier in the day, and then all the anticipation of the train itself, the telegraph could have been dead for up to two hours and nobody any the wiser. 'An' if yuh're talkin' about some damn' posse,' Tyler went on, 'I'd not hold out a lot o' hope fer that, Marshal, for none of 'em in these parts look to have the stomach fer it, an' any as does prob'ly wouldn't bother to ride. Don't take it too much to heart, Nightgall. Me an' ol' Gates here kin give yuh plenty to chew on if yuh're so determined, but allers bear in mind it could be worse. It could be Burnett.' The words hammered brutally at Nightgall as they were intended to do, and his big hand tightened on the butt of the long pistol.

Impatiently the albino shouted, 'Jes' piss off, Nightgall an' quit yore gran'standin'!'

'Better back off as they want, Mr Nightgall,'

called Asherton. As far as he was concerned there was no way out, but he added, 'My man, Gilby, is in there dead.' Asherton truly looked shattered, very pale and somehow shrunken, but Nightgall realized that in all likelihood it was not on his own account, but out of compassion for the man dead inside the bank, and real fear about the survival of the other, Peters; men who both had dependents, bank clerks who, earlier that same morning, had simply left their homes and come to their work as usual. Asherton quite clearly was already assuming as his own the burden of responsibility for these events no matter what the circumstances had been.

'I'm pullin' back now,' called Nightgall, and he showed himself then, though still with drawn pistol, but unquestionably backing away. The four of them still stood, a small, wary tableau, in the yard with the horses, though now the albino was concerned with steadying one of the animals that had begun tossing its head. Nightgall passed slowly from their view, pacing backwards, knowing that he would be best not to try anything too fly, for they might yet choose to come walking the horses out of the yard and herding the men from the bank ahead of them.

But away down the length of these back lots in this back street, just about where Liz Ellwood's place was, a man came limping into view, drawn no doubt by the sound of the earlier gunfire, a man holding a shotgun and who immediately raised a hand when he identified the distant Nightgall. Nightgall made some violent motions with one hand, pointing in an exaggerated way towards the yard at the bank and was gratified to see Gus Forbes go limping away out of sight again. Nightgall had cleared away from the yard by a good margin while still keeping his attention on it, and felt he had reached a place where he could wait, in fact beyond the other livery corral, near the barn at the back of it and near also to Gollin's. It seemed to him a long time though before anything else happened, but when it did it was with an eruption of movement that made even Nightgall blink. First, before he saw anything, there came the sound of the horses. The men must have rowelled them quite savagely for they were going at a good clip when they came bursting into view, Tyler first, then Gates, his hat still bouncing between his shoulder blades, white hair prominent, hauling the horses' heads around, away from the direction they knew Nightgall to have gone. As soon as that happened, Nightgall knelt and pistol bucking, banged a shot away, the blue gunsmoke acrid in his nostrils, and then he was up again and running, firing a second time. They were quirting their mounts vigorously, canvas bags bouncing either side as they went, and even as Nightgall ran, were hauling up again, obviously seeking an early opening that would lead them on to Main. Puzzled at first, Nightgall then caught sight of Forbes, shotgun to his shoulder, even as he heard the full-throated explosion of the gun, not effective at the range, but quite enough to cause the mounted men to seek a quick way out. Tyler and Gates were entering a side alley when Nightgall knelt, steadied, and blasted another shot, and this time he heard the smack as he hit Gates' trailing horse, and then they were both gone urgently down the alley. Gone too, was Forbes. Nightgall ran on but his chest was heaving and he knew that by the time he himself got on to Main, whatever the situation was, he would not be in good shape for shooting. Indeed, when he did reach Main he was down to a walk, but was at least gratified to see that if there had been any curious citizens around when the riders appeared, they had sensibly made themselves scarce.

Tyler and Gates were there though, Tyler still mounted but turned around, horse prancing about, while the albino's mount was down, raking its back legs, screaming, head up trying to rise, blood all over its neck, the albino, covered in dust from the street, where he had apparently taken a fall, was trying to free the canvas sacks. Tyler, shouting 'Leave 'em! Mount up behind!' saw Nightgall arrive some sixty feet from them and let go a booming shot but the horse was still on the move and the slug was well astray. The albino was not about to give up on pulling the sacks from his struggling horse in spite of Tyler's bawling at him, so Nightgall shot at him and the slug actually thumped the bag out of the albino's grasp, but still it would not come free. Gates, his pinkish eyes blazing, came part-way to his feet and drew his pistol. Nightgall shuffled back to the mouth of the alley by which they had all entered Main, for they both began shooting at him, Tyler now having settled his horse down. But Tyler was still bawling at the albino to forget the sacks and climb up on his horse. Gates' horse was still screaming and trying to rise, raising clouds of dust, and finally Gates went to its head, held the long-barrelled pistol there and shot it. The horse gave one final rear of the head and flopped down, quiet. Then the albino crouched behind the animal and once more began struggling to release the sacks and after a moment gave a triumphant shout and dragged them clear.

'Christ! Come on!' Tyler shouted.

Nightgall then went forward a few short paces, drew down and fired and in the swirl of blue smoke around him saw the albino knocked back and, half-turning, fall to his knees, then get up and lean, clutching, against Tyler's horse. Nightgall shot again and this time, although it was not hit, Tyler's horse went skitter-stepping sideways and the albino fell down once again. But Nightgall slipped back to the cover of the alley, for that had been his fifth shot and the carry chamber had not been loaded. As quickly as he could, but with care, too, he began to reload the big pistol. When he looked again Tyler had no pistol in his hand and was leaning down, grasping one of Gates' wrists, endeavouring to help him up, but horse and wounded man were both moving awkwardly, and it was quite plain that Gates was not going to be able to get up, and certainly not with the fallen sacks.

Nightgall knew that this was his chance, perhaps the only one he was likely to get. Mercifully, any people who were still inside nearby buildings were choosing to stay there and those who had been welcoming the train, though no doubt by now very much aware of what was happening, if any of them were watching, then they were doing so discreetly, from a considerable distance.

Tyler let go of Gates who somehow had drawn his pistol again and had cleared himself away from Tyler's horse. Maybe the albino knew that it was all done with, that he was never going to be able to climb up on Tyler's nor any other horse, for now, a lot of blood on his shirt and on his left hand, which at some stage he had pressed to the wound, he focused completely on Nightgall, and in his single-minded, face-flooding rage, started towards him. The albino, coming unsteadily, closing the range, might have had but one live round remaining and wanted to make it count, but now he was between Tyler and Nightgall, rendering Tyler for the moment ineffective. Nightgall had seldom seen such an advance, never seen such raw hatred as now fired the eyes of the white-haired man in his ragged clothing, coming in a lurching walk with a purpose to kill him. When Gates did stop, and raised his pistol, Nightgall, having left it to the last possible instant, shot him, hit him hard near the breastbone and thumped him backwards and the shock of the hit caused Gates to discharge his own pistol in a spurt of smoke and a leap of dust as the lead went into the street. The albino fell down, tried to rise, fell again, dust and smoke still hanging above him. Tyler shouted and fired, wheeling his horse, and Nightgall, perhaps incautiously, kept moving forward, determined to bring Tyler down, but as he swung the long barrel up, stopped, blinked his eyes, shook his head, for suddenly horse and rider had lost their clarity and indeed for a moment Nightgall saw little more than greyness and at once began backing off, firing blind. His calves struck the boardwalk behind him and he all but fell. Then his vision cleared. Tyler, seeing something was wrong, thinking perhaps that at some stage Nightgall had been hit, gave a whoop and got the horse around with the obvious intent of riding full at the marshal.

The thunderclap of Gus Forbes' shotgun was the next thing heard, probably right throughout Wheeler, and while Forbes was still too far away for his shot to have any effect on Tyler, beyond the sting of a few lead pellets, spreading as they went, it did again unsettle the man's horse, causing it this time to go up with back arched and all but unseat its rider. Flung sideways, he swung a leg back in a partial dismount rather than be thrown, and then had to go on with it and jump to the street as Nightgall yelled and fired, though with his vision still slightly blurred, so that Tyler's horse went bucking away, the sacks lifting and falling at each leap, and Tyler now afoot and wanting to distance himself from Nightgall and get no closer to Forbes who, gun broken open, was obviously reloading, gained the opposite boardwalk, then turned and ran down a sidestreet. From earlier calling all the shots, it had now gone badly wrong in a real hurry for Tyler, but he was still apparently unhurt, and though separated from the horse, still very dangerous indeed.

Nightgall waved a hand to Forbes, signalling him to keep back, to stay near Liz. Thankfully, there was no sign of her. Nightgall pressed the horned palm of one hand to his forehead, closing his eyes several times quickly. His sight now seemed to have returned near to normal. From his distance Gus Forbes watched him fixedly for a moment longer, then went limping back towards Liz Ellwood's shop. In the opposite direction, one or two people had begun to come out on the boardwalks, but Nightgall waved them back also. Whatever happened he wanted freedom of movement to get on after Tyler and nobody to get in the way of the shooting. One face he did seek, however, was Asherton's and when he saw that the banker was indeed there, looking in his direction, he beckoned, indicating the fallen money sacks. Gun still drawn, anxious to be on the move, nonetheless he waited for Asherton and Peters to start walking up Main and then, at a half-jog, he himself crossed Main and entered the street down which Tyler had gone.

This was the street where the lumber yard was, where in darkness, pretending to quarrel, the men had waited to trap Nightgall; men he had not known and had not seen again in Wheeler. Now, at the corner where the lumber yard was he looked about him but could see nothing at all of Tyler. He wondered if he ought to go searching among the stacks of lumber before going anywhere else. Now, that would be a deadly game, every corner, every narrow gap between the stacks bringing the threat of Tyler, waiting. At close quarters, without warning, anything could happen. Yet Nightgall came again to his recollection of Stokes at the barn, a place which had seized his attention as it had been intended to do. Perhaps this lumber yard was another of those places, where he might, in taking necessary caution, waste much time. Another thought came to him. Would Tyler seek to mingle in the crowd at the depot, perhaps even board the train? Probably not, for there would be the risk of being taken, even shot by the railroad guards, for by now his identity and his appearance would be widely known. Corrado's? Would he try to get inside Corrado's? Again Nightgall thought not. Which left – what? The rag-taggle of yards and refuse dumps along this street that ran parallel to Main, the barrels, boxes, the few wagons, the many outbuildings, a couple of small corrals. Nightgall now began to walk this dangerous back street. Eventually it would bring him nearer the depot where the crowd was, and from where now, he could see smoke and steam going up from the standing locomotive; and soon after that it would bring him to the back of Corrado's and beyond. Fleetingly, Dobrey's face came to mind and Nightgall felt thankful for the presence of the stolid Forbes with his shotgun along at Liz Ellwood's. But somewhere in this unsavoury jumble along the backs of the buildings of Main, he felt certain that Tyler would be lying in wait, so there was nothing for it but to tempt the man to make a move. On he went, slow pace after slow pace, looking left and right, the sun beating down, sometimes glancing over his shoulder, cautious, watchful, a fist clenched somewhere inside his belly, knowing that the first shot must surely come from Tyler and that it might be a clean hit.

At Liz Ellwood's, Polly Marchant, her anger long spent, her face bathed clean of tears and then dried by the very woman she had set out to cut, to disfigure with a razor, sat with a coffee mug clasped in both her hands, the hot drink richly laced with brandy.

'Drink now,' Liz had said, 'then we'll talk.'

At Corrado's, the man himself, cigar clamped in his teeth, moved among the many empty tables in the dingy atmosphere of the Silver Cat. Dobrey, alone at his green baize, under a lamp, was thoughtfully cutting and shuffling bright cards. Court was occupied in solemnly wiping the long, polished bar, needlessly now, filling time, wondering where the hell Polly had got to.

Those who often set up a game in the back room at Frater's were there now, but idling, not playing, not saying a lot either, listening for more gunfire.

'So what d'yuh reckon on Nightgall now?'

'It ain't done yet. That Tyler's a bad bastard.'

'I dunno about Nightgall no more.'

'Tyler might be a bad bastard an' a han'ful, but he ain't this Burnett.'

Nightgall, in the revealing bright sun, his foreshortened shadow sharp and clear, walked steadily on.

When it did come it was sudden and very fast, Tyler standing up from behind the shelter of a heavy, flat-deck wagon, blazing at Nightgall amid a gauze of blue gunsmoke, but jumpy, maybe, and carried away and shooting too fast, yet one big, lethal slug nipping the broad brim of the marshal's hat. Nightgall, firmly controlling the impulse to dodge away, stood still and fired, and though Tyler was on the move, believed that he had hit him, for the man's left leg buckled and he went partially down, then recovered, retreating among some sacks of fly-ridden garbage out behind a cafe. Somebody opened a back door, then promptly shut it.

Nightgall shouted, 'Nowhere to go, Tyler!' He squatted, left knee and left hand resting on the ground and he could hear Tyler moving and an empty can was kicked and went rolling, but from where he was he could no longer see him. Nightgall remained thus, propped on the ground, and again raised the long pistol, slowly tracking along from the place where he had last seen Tyler, then brought it just as deliberately back again. When Tyler moved once more, hastening further away and definitely limping, Nightgall saw him and he himself rose and jogged off in pursuit. At the corner of an alley Tyler paused and shot again at Nightgall, but too high, and closing the distance between them, Nightgall could now make out a reddish patch high up on the man's left thigh, before Tyler spun away around the corner and so again passed from view, obviously heading back towards Main, perhaps to seek there his abandoned horse. Nightgall did not follow him directly but vaulted a heap of stinking, decomposing garbage and went in through the back door of the cafe. A cook in a greasy apron dropped a skillet and backed off when the marshal came in, seeming to fill the place with his bulk, a fearsome sight, sweating and dusty, with a hellbound look about him, and the great pistol in one hand. With a sweep of his other arm he went on through a bead curtain and beyond that, through between the deserted tables to a door with yellow and white checkered glass that would let him out on to Main. He wrenched the door open and went boldly on to the boardwalk.

Tyler, though wounded in the leg had not wasted any time, but was going at a limping jog up the middle of the street towards where the horse still was, calmer now, its reins hanging; but glancing back he saw where Nightgall had come out. Tyler slowed and fired, glass somewhere behind Nightgall smashing, as he went down off the boardwalk, moving determinedly after Tyler. Nightgall though, after all the hurried movements, the urgency and the tension, was beginning to feel the pinch quite badly now, his breathing shorter, and a burning down inside him every time he drew breath. He knew that his general condition would not make for good shooting but there was no option but to go on. He could not afford to allow Tyler to reach the horse. People were beginning to reappear on all parts of Main, brought there at last by natural and compelling curiosity, and some were getting imprudently close to where the action was. So when Tyler, having apparently concluded that, his wounded leg sorely restricting his movements, he was not going to get away from the big man doggedly following him without standing and actually shooting him, turned and prepared to meet Nightgall head-on. This, the marshal knew, was the most dangerous time, not only for himself but for others who might have ventured too close, so he resolved that this would be it. It had to be got done with. It was him or Tyler. He would close the range and keep closing it and sooner or later one of them would be hit. On he went, even seeing Tyler reloading his pistol, seeing him finish doing it and almost casually raise the weapon; but Nightgall went forward inexorably, eyes fixed unswervingly on Tyler, thankful for clear vision now, a big, darkly-dressed man, grey hair curling at his neck and above his ears. Tyler shot, missed. Still Nightgall came on. He could see sudden uncertainty now in Tyler. Again Tyler's hand holding the pistol was coming down, but Nightgall, extending his arm, blasted his own long pistol at him and that was it, that was a hit, Tyler thumped away, elbows suddenly held in, awkwardly, crouchingly, to his solar plexus; then on his knees, his body swaying, a shriek of agony torn from him, eyes already filled with pain and fear; filled too, with the awesome sight of the big bastard still coming in at him, fogged again in gunsmoke, striding in upon another thunderclap, and Tyler, hit hard a second time, was down fast as though kicked by a stallion, in a tumble of dust and blood and raggy clothing, dead before the shadow of the walking man came across him.

Nightgall lay back in one of the big chairs at Liz

Ellwood's. It was later in the day and he had now done all that he could usefully do in the aftermath of the determined attempt on the Wheeler bank. His whole body was aching, his left knee in particular, and his head was throbbing. She had given him coffee laced substantially with brandy as she had done for Polly, and now for a little time he drifted between two worlds. Polly Marchant had gone, poor sad Polly. Court had been sent for because there was really no one else, but before he had let him anywhere near the girl, Nightgall, towering above him, had said, 'Touch her again in anger, Court, drunk or sober, an' you'll not lift another glass with either hand for a good twelvemonth. An' pass that same word around up there at Corrado's, because by God I mean it.'

The first train to Wheeler had been and now had gone again and the excitement which had been expected and which ordinarily might have followed this landmark in the history of the town had not eventuated, at least nearly not to the extent that had been contemplated. There had been dead men on Main and another, a young and well-known one, inside the Wheeler bank. The dead from Main had been taken across to the jail-house and there, for the time being, laid side by side on the cold floor of one of the cells.

'But not for too long, with any luck,' Nightgall had said. 'The place stinks bad enough now.' And upon coming out of the cell he had, out of habit, locked the barred door behind him and had joined the little rush of subdued laughter from those who had done the carrying.

The dead man at the bank, Gilby, had been carried to his home, and there, both Asherton and Nightgall had spent some time with the widow. Nightgall had left Asherton there.

The albino had perhaps not cut the telegraph wires much before entering the bank, so Tyler's words on that subject, to Asherton and Peters, were now revealed to have been big-mouthing. There were in fact two breaches, one about a mile short of Wheeler, the other a similar distance beyond, and a party which went out for the purpose was able to restore the wire link in not much more than a couple of hours.

So, unburdened for the time being, Nightgall lay half sleeping in the warmth of the late afternoon. He did not hear anyone come in but he smelled him, smelled the sweat and mothballs, and opened his eyes to see Evans in the room, and even though it was still daylight, Liz, for some reason had lit a lamp and was holding it. He was struggling to rise but she pressed her other hand against his shoulder.

'No. Please. Let Mr Evans look at your eyes.' She thereupon held the lamp closer, apparently obeying Evans' wish, and Evans himself, one grubby finger on Nightgall's leathern cheek, pulling down, and another on the eyelid, pulling up, examined first one eye and then the other. Nightgall discovered, not with surprise, that Evans had quite foul breath, too.

'Well?' Nightgall demanded when Evans seemingly had finished.

'It might well have been concussion,' Evans said. 'At this time anyway, Marshal, you are in no fit condition to do what you are accustomed to doing.'

He asked about the loss of vision and when Nightgall looked sourly at Liz, she said, 'Gus Forbes realized what happened on Main. The albino might have killed you then.'

'He was comin' a-purpose to do that,' said Nightgall grittily.

'My advice is that you take things a lot easier, Mr Nightgall,' Evans said. Diplomatically, he refrained from mentioning age for he had not at all liked the looks that the Wheeler marshal had been giving him.

When Evans had gone, Liz extinguished the lamp, opened another window and wafted a dish-towel around to freshen the air.

'That man sure stinks,' Nightgall said.

'Nonetheless, what he told you makes sense. It makes sense to me, anyway.'

She had told him everything that had happened when Polly Marchant had come into the shop, and now said, 'Poor Polly.'

'Poor Polly could well have opened up your face from hairline to jaw,' said Nightgall, 'an' might have done if old Gus hadn't walked in when he did.'

'In my whole life,' said Liz, 'I have never been as

pleased to see another human being.'

'I'll not tell him that,' muttered Nightgall, 'for it might give the old buzzard ideas.'

Though usually he would have preached puritanical principles on the subject, he did not resist more brandy., this time a tumblerful, neat, and surprisingly, sat sipping it with some evidence of pleasure. Maybe it had been the brandy, she thought afterwards, because for the first time he began to talk a little about his past and about some of the things that he knew were said by some in Wheeler behind twitching curtains after he had gone by. As though he had simply been muttering to himself, he said then, 'All about Burnett.'

Scarcely daring to open her mouth, she had nonetheless asked, very quietly, 'Who *is* he? Who *is* Burnett?'

She thought at first that he had lost interest and fallen asleep but after a long pause, he said, 'His name's not Burnett. That's a name he took.'

'Took?' She could not now see his leathery face in all its detail, for the day's shadows were lengthening and the room was becoming darker. 'He took the name Burnett?'

Nightgall passed one callused hand across his face and she saw his chest rise as he drew in a long breath.

'It's a long time in the past,' he said, his voice much lower than usual, so that she had to listen carefully in order to catch the words; and as though he had changed tack completely, he said, 'I told you that she died? Gemma?'

'Yes.'

'What I didn't tell you was that she was shot.' Liz closed her own eyes briefly, not daring now to interrupt. 'It happened in a place called St Aubin. I was marshal there, too. We'd been out, the two of us, to spend some time with friends. It was near midnight when we went up the walk to the front porch of our house. A man named Archer, from a bad, messy business some time before, was there, come to square it with me as he saw it, a man I'd long stopped even thinkin' about. That was a bad mistake, an' at that time I didn't even have the excuse of age. He fired but Gemma took the bullet. She had no chance. It hit her above the left eye. No chance. An' Archer, that bastard, he got clean away. So there wasn't even that satisfaction.'

She found that she had covered her face with her hands.

'Then *he* is Burnett?'

'No. Oh no, not Archer.' He paused as if weighing whether or not to continue, but then he said, 'Gemma's name, before we were married, was Burnett.'

'Then ...'

'He's our son. My son.' She could not take it in at once, staring at him, but he still seemed somnolent, not noticing. 'As a boy, he worshipped Gemma. When Rafe Archer's bullet killed her, shot her when it was me he'd wanted dead, he killed something deep inside the boy, too. We'd never been that close, him an' me.' She could not decide whether or not she did see a sardonic twist to his lip. 'I do things my way where I pay the piper. But anyway, he blamed me fair an' square for what had happened to his mother. One thing led to another an' within a year he'd slung his warbag an' lit out, an' in poorish company at that. I have to say it, admit that he went to the bad. The drink got a-hold, one part, so I did hear.' This time she was sure he almost smiled. 'Folks ain't slow to fetch the bad news. But whatever happened, as time went on he seems to have got the notion that he was the man to finish what Rafe Archer had set out to do. Bragged a lot about it, an' that came back on the wind, too; though from near the start he'd taken her name, Burnett, so as time passed there'd have been few, maybe none, who'd have made the connection 'tween me an' him.'

She knew that she had no need to explain the kinds of things that had been muttered about in Wheeler.

'That's the reason you left Argon. He'd come there to find you?'

He shook his head. 'Not to find me, he didn't. Come by chance as far as that went. No, he came into Argon for some woman there. Could be there still for all I know. So there I was an' there he was, with his dire promises all come beforehand, on the wind.' So now it had been said; something else, perhaps the last thing, washed clean between himself and Liz. He thought he could stay right here in this soft, capacious chair, and sleep for a month.

The burying done, the town had fallen quiet, almost as though, treading softly, it was of a mind to seek some kind of forgiveness for the unspeakable occurrences in its midst. The days went by and very gradually a feeling of normality came back, though the unwanted memories were there and the mounds in the burial-places were still fresh. Other trains came hauling long, flat-decked wagons bearing steel rails and sleepers for the further progress of the track beyond the town. The people who remained in Wheeler, whose livelihood it was, resumed the day-by-day currency and commerce of their lives, ranch wagons and buckboards coming and going, lifting fine dust, and some of the railroad men still came regularly too, and the big marshal resumed his regular pacing of the boardwalks of Main. The murmurings about him had ceased.

Liz was alone one early evening, however, when someone rapped sharply at the back porch.

In the spill of light from the doorway stood Forbes. She invited him inside but he declined, looking decidedly uncomfortable, once even glancing behind him as though he might have expected to see someone else there in the gloom. Probably because he looked as though he did not want to ask outright, she smiled faintly and said, 'He's not here right now, Gus.'

He shifted his weight off his bad leg.

'Been over to the jail but there's no lamps nowhere.'

'He's likely down talking with Mr Asherton.' Something was wrong. She could have sensed it even if the man had not looked so uncomfortable. 'What is it? What's happened?'

Forbes said: 'Look, there's been things said that might be the truth but prob'ly ain't, leastways not all of the truth. You know that, an' I reckon I don't have to go jawin' on about it. But – well, one of 'em has took shape, Liz. There's a man come into Wheeler not an hour since, that Nightgall ought to know about.'

A kind of chill swept through her. Forbes, by Nightgall's account, was not a man who was easily rattled. She knew she must allow him to go on, yet in one way she was afraid of hearing what it was he had come to say.

'Who? What man?'

He looked at her levelly. 'Feller by the name o' Burnett.'

She drew her breath in quickly as the shock of it struck home at her, and put one hand on the doorframe. Then, 'Where is he, now?'

'Far as I know he's still up at Corrado's. By the looks, he seemed to know Ash Dobrey. Or mebbe, by this, he's gone to Frater's.'

'You've actually seen him? What does he look like?'

'Not old. Touchin' thirty I'd guess, but with a kinda … older face. Big man, tall, strong lookin', an' I'd say somewhat of a handful.'

So it had happened. The good days of the earlier past were all for naught, the good days to come, an illusion. The nightmare had materialized. After a moment or two she managed to say, 'Thank you for coming, Gus. I'll tell him as soon as he comes.' He touched his old hat and went limping away out of the reach of the light. Slowly she closed the door.

She had found him at the back of Frater's, he having gone there, as she watched, to install his dusty black horse in the barn.

Inside the barn a single low lamp was burning, hanging from a hook, and outside, shadows were made deep and sharp by the moon.

At her soft step he had turned with astonishing speed and the great eye of the pistol was already centred on her.

'Go ahead,' she told him, 'it would be easy.' She was almost totally in shadow, wearing a dark blue cloak with a hood that was pulled up, and at the sound of her voice he slowly put the pistol back in its holster. She knew she was risking everything, risking herself, risking losing Nightgall. At his drawing of the pistol he had stepped back a pace and now remained there steeped in shadow.

'Who are you?' His voice was hard, penetrating, the echo of another voice.

'Liz Ellwood.'

He must have been well and early briefed.

'So,' Burnett said, 'you're his woman.'

'I'm his woman.' She found it very easy to say.

'I bet he doesn't know you're here.'

'Of course not.'

'Of course not. Pride. Pride with a hard mouth an' never lookin' away,' Burnett said. 'Why are you here, then?'

'To ask you to go.'

'Just like that,' he said. He shifted slightly and the light caught his dark, handsome features and in that instant she glimpsed the youth of Nightgall. 'The great Nightgall,' he said. 'The great marshal. He told you all of his history? I reckon he would have, at that.'

'Yes, he's told me. But I can't, I'll never be able to understand, in spite of it, why you should fix your hate on *him*. He made no excuses, to me; simply said what it was that happened. How could it have been his fault?'

'Fault or no fault, this or that, she's no less dead. Over an' over she asked him, pleaded with him to give it up, go away, to get someplace where he wouldn't be a target. If we'd done it, gone far enough, we'd have shaken it all, maybe taken a different name. But he wouldn't hear any of it, so it stuck to us like a goddam' burr. That's why *I* threw the name away, for the first two men I killed, I killed because o' that name. They came to kill a name an' instead I killed *them*. It was the name that killed *her*.' He was still half in shadow but the dull yellow light was catching the brim of his hat on one side, one hand, and the butt of the heavy pistol jutting below his right hip.

'I can't make that different, neither can he; nor you, now.'

'Yeah, I can make it different.'

'He's no longer young. He took a bad blow and sometimes his sight goes; and he has a hurt knee he thinks I don't know about.'

'He's had a blindness all his life, that man,' said Burnett. 'Well, I've come here a-purpose. I won't go 'til I've done this, brushed the burr off for good an' all.'

'He might kill *you*.'

'He might. If he does, then I'll have killed him just the same.'

'Or he might simply leave, as he left Argon.'

'No, not this time. Pride. An' you're here.'

Then she was angry, unable to contain it, her voice low but almost spitting the words at him.

'Go on then. When the light comes, get your killing done. Kill him in the street where all of Wheeler can see you do it. Kill him, the old man, the half-blind man, trying not to limp. Do it! Soon, nobody will remember how uneven a match it really was, because you'll not have to face any of the people here again. No, you'll be gone, hiding behind your false name, big man, big talk. *See him, Burnett? He killed the great Nightgall*. And only I and the people here in Wheeler will know the truth of it.'

'You'd best go.'

'Oh, I'm going. I'm going back to wait for my man. Nightgall. I'd have the name, too, if he'd ever asked me, but there seemed no need. We just got along. It was good to be with a good man. It—' She shook her head as though to clear it, then turned quickly and went hurrying away; but in the moment of her turning the hood fell back and for the first time he saw her face clear and clean in the bright moon and almost gasped, as though he might have seen a ghost. But she was gone, her cloak billowing, her steps quickening, vanishing. Burnett stood stock still looking into the moon-barred night long after she had left him.

It had been late when finally Nightgall had returned and she had waited up for him and he had known that something was wrong as soon as he had looked at her. He had hung his hat on a peg and wearily passed a large hand across his face.

Now, in the early morning, every look, every inflection was still as clear in her mind as it had been then.

'Gus Forbes came here earlier this evening. Burnett is in Wheeler.' For some reason that she herself could not fathom, she could not make herself say 'your son'. The man was Burnett, long talked about behind hands; Burnett, the long shadow, and still so, in spite of the fact that she had, but an hour or two past, stood close to him in the dappled shadows of the barn behind Frater's.

Nightgall seemed to take it calmly enough, resignedly perhaps.

'He's certain? Gus? Certain it's him?'

'He said he was certain.'

'Where is he?'

'When Gus saw him he was in Corrado's. Probably by now he's at Frater's.' He nodded, then sat down on a sofa, looking tired. 'What will you do?'

'Do? Well, what I won't do is what I did at Argon. I won't leave this town because he's come here.'

'You'll talk with him?'

'Talk? Liz, I don't reckon it's a matter of talk. All the talk was done with long ago 'tween me an' him. So if he's here in Wheeler, then he came because he knew for sure I was here. Somebody in the town told him where I was. I could sit here makin' all sorts of guesses about that all night but it probably doesn't matter anyway.'

She felt unnaturally chilled. 'So there's no more to be said. Will you go now? Tonight?'

He shook his head. 'Never did fancy a night shoot.' He looked up at her. 'Besides, I doubt I'd manage to lift the pistol.'

She was awake but her eyes were still closed when she felt the bed move slightly as he left it and she heard him padding around no doubt collecting the clean clothes she had laid out for him; then she heard the bedroom door close quietly. Thereafter, the occasional sound reached her. She turned over. The little carriage-clock on her dresser said 7.50 a.m. She thought she would lie there a little while and leave him to his devices. She could by now have recited his routine. The privy door in the yard banged. Presently a clanging noise told her he was preparing a bath. He would heat water, take a bath, washing with fastidious care, and when he had dried himself, put on clean underclothing and shirt. Once he had both astonished and appalled her by saying in a most matter-of-fact way: 'If there's a shoot to come an' you know it, if you go clean, clean skin, fresh clothes, then if you get hit there's a touch less chance of some infection bein' driven in.' It had seemed to her so professionally cold-blooded that she had looked away from him and shuddered. And he had a thing about not touching food before going out when he knew there was to be real danger; a sip or two of water perhaps, but not much of that either. He would then strip the long pistol and make quite sure that all its parts were functioning properly, clean and oil the big weapon and perhaps this time, even load the carry-chamber. 'Six beans in the wheel for once.' She could almost hear his hard voice saying it.

She swung her legs out of the warmth of the bed and slipped into her wine-coloured robe.

Nightgall was in the kitchen rinsing a water

glass. He was fully dressed, ready for the street, hat and all, with the pistol slung and the old holster thonged down. To her unspoken question he said, 'Goin' over to my place. There's a few things to tidy up.' At the door he paused as though to say something else and she looked at him expectantly, but in the finish he simply turned and left.

She realized that as she was standing there she was gripping the edge of the table. Never for a second had she doubted that he would go. He was the marshal here. Whoever came to the town must feel themselves open to his scrutiny. There were no exceptions. He would return to his own place first though, just as he had said, and probably would go up to the jail office, and because he was a careful and dutiful and methodical man, there attend to a dozen matters of routine, maybe pass as long as a couple of hours at such tasks and then, when he was ready, go out and walk up Main, where everybody could see him, looking for Burnett. She felt as though she wanted to dress quickly and go after him right now, while he would still be over at the jail-house, for there were surely a hundred and one things yet to be said that soon might never be said. But she did not. It was not her place. No matter about anything else or what anybody might think, afterwards, it was not her place. Somehow she must manage to go about her normal business, open the shop, try to put up a pretence, stupid though it might seem, that this was a day like any other.

When he came out at last into the brightness of the street it was mid-morning. He had no way of knowing how many of the citizens of Wheeler knew that Burnett was here, and why, but he did not by any action or by anything in his demeanour, betray to any who did know, what he himself was thinking. Outwardly all was as usual. He went striding along the boardwalk, the darkly-clad marshal, unhurried, relaxed, on one of his routine walks, courteously passing a word here, a word there in the warm morning. At a certain place he paused, looking at the street. Over there was where the albino had died trying to come in awkwardly and stupidly on to a long pistol, consumed by his rage, the arbiter of his own destruction. And further along, just out there in fact, near the middle of Main, Tyler, the pock-marked man, had been shot to death; already hit once, had turned finally to face what was to come by waiting for the advancing Nightgall. Now Tyler's chestnut horse and all his possessions together with the saddle and the other belongings of Gates were in the custody of Asherton, to be sold by him to defray the expenses of the burials, the remainder of the money to be awarded the young widow of the bank clerk, Gilby. Nightgall himself had been occupied to some extent during the past hour and a half in documenting all of that in detail, for it had been the fruits of his night-meeting with Asherton. He walked on. Presently, across on the opposite side of the street he saw Gus Forbes in his doorway and he paused and gave a look that the sharp-minded Forbes read instantly; Forbes shook his head. No sighting of Burnett by him, anyway. Nightgall walked on.

When he looked in at Corrado's he did not ask for Burnett, knowing that if he were there he would have been forewarned of the marshal's approach and would have been in the long bar and nowhere else, had he been in the place at all. There would be no acts of subterfuge, no dodging about in this affair. The two of them would simply meet somewhere. However he did pause for a word with Ash Dobrey, who did not particularly wish to see or hear him.

'Polly Marchant,' Nightgall said. 'If Court hasn't passed the word, then hear it now. If more harm should come to Polly, I've told Court I'll break his hands. If anybody else should have any ideas about it and not take due note of what I've said, or forget themselves, I'll be the next goddam' customer in through that door. If I have to do that an' I find, say, that you're involved, you might thereafter need to deal them damn' things with your teeth. And don't ever go anywhere near Mrs Ellwood again.' Dobrey's eyes narrowed, so Nightgall said, 'You want to push it, make an issue, there's no place like this one an' no time like the present.'

Meantime Corrado had drawn nearer, chewing cigar smoke.

'Heard there was a feller askin' for yuh Marshal.'

'I heard that too,' said Nightgall. 'In fact that's why I'm out an' about, so if he wants to find me, he won't need to look under anything or behind anything. There I'll be, right in plain view.' He strolled out of the Silver Cat and when the batwings were still wagging behind him, Corrado, first drawing on his cigar, said, 'Was it you sent for him? Burnett?'

Dobrey, still drawn with shock and anger, said 'Maybe.'

'I sure as Jesus hope yuh know what yuh're doin',' said Corrado. He did not like to have Nightgall putting in sudden appearances in this saloon.

Nightgall, on the boardwalk, almost collided with Polly Marchant and he stood for a moment looking down at her, holding her shoulders very lightly.

'You all right, Polly?'

'Yeah, I guess.'

'Court won't lay a hand on you no more,' he said 'Ash Dobrey's got the word, too, from me, plain as plain.'

'Good, I hope you did give it to the bastard straight.'

'You sure could say that,' said Nightgall. Then 'Polly, why don't you get out, go to some other place, some better town?'

'Where? Is there one?'

'How the hell do I know?' he said. 'There might be.'

He walked along and into Frater's and there he did ask for Burnett. They said they had not seen the man whom Nightgall perhaps thought was the stranger named Burnett (for he had given them no such name) since the previous night. But this particular man did have a horse in their barn.

Nightgall thereupon went to Frater's barn but there was no horse there. It occurred to him then that in earlier days, had he but known soon enough, Gollin's Trading Company would have proved to be a rewarding place to begin seeking certain men; so he went across Main and into Gollin's, but Gollin denied having seen Burnett, though he had heard that such a man was in Wheeler. Nightgall, glimpsing Crake 'way down among the merchandise called to him and Crake came uncertainly up to where Nightgall and Gollin were.

'I seen a man ridin' out. Ridin' out in no great hurry, like he might have some long ways to go.'

'When? Today?'

'Not long after sun-up,' said Crake. 'Tall, hard-lookin' feller on a black. Come from in back o' Frater's by the looks.'

Nightgall stared at Crake. There seemed no reason to disbelieve him. In any case, Crake was mortally afraid of Nightgall, and his last wish would be to be caught out by the marshal in a silly lie.

Nightgall left Gollin's and went back out on to Main. Corrado was now standing just inside the batwing doors of the Silver Cat. Nightgall stared hard at him and Corrado withdrew. The marshal paced along the boardwalk, going easily, not yielding to the sharp, darting pain in his left leg. Going on by the office of the stage-line he raised a hand to Forbes, walked on towards his destination, Liz Ellwood's shop.

Liz, for all her efforts, unable to settle, had been standing in her doorway and finally saw him, though still some good long distance off, coming in her direction. With some uncanny insight and an almost draining relief, she thought that she knew what it was that he was coming to tell her. She drew back inside the cool, familiar shop. He was alive. He was coming back. This time there had been no gunfire unexplained, no dreadful, stomach-gripping hiatus. She closed her eyes. What was she to make of this man who would never, ever change or stop being what he was? Brave and cautious, sometimes foolhardy, finicky, sardonic, loving, and often, she thought, impossible; too old, too long bound to what he did ever to turn back. He no longer had a choice in the matter, so truly there was nothing else for it but to go on. He was a man who was his own prisoner and his own jailer; but from now until the end of it, he was also hers.

He was Nightgall.